THE DORYMAN

Maura Hanrahan

THE DORYMAN

BY MAURA HANRAHAN

Flanker Press Ltd.
St. John's, Newfoundland
2003

National Library of Canada Cataloguing in Publication

Hanrahan, Maura, 1963-
    The doryman : a novel / Maura Hanrahan.

ISBN 1-894463-40-4

    1. Hanrahan, Richard--Fiction.   2. Windstorms--Newfoundland--
Fiction. I. Title.

PS8565.A5875D67 2003   C813'.6   C2003-904533-1

Copyright © 2003 by Maura Hanrahan

Printed in Canada

First printing September 2003
Second printing July 2004

Cover design by Dale Wilson

Flanker Press Ltd.
P.O. Box 2522, Station C
St. John's, Newfoundland A1C 6K1
Toll Free: 1-866-739-4420
Telephone: (709) 739-4477
Fax: (709) 739-4420

E-mail: info@flankerpress.com
www.flankerpress.com

Canada

We acknowledge the financial support of the Government of Canada through the Book Publishing Industry Development Program (BPIDP) for our publishing program.

This book is written in loving memory of my grandfather
Richard
and is dedicated to my uncle Vince

Maura Catherine Hanrahan
August, 2003

Author's Note

This book is a fictionalized account of my grandfather's life in the Grand Banks schooner fishery of the early twentieth century. It is based on first-hand accounts from family members, and family stories, and supplemented by articles in the *Daily News*, the *Evening Telegram*, the *Halifax Herald*, and the *Berwick Register* of the day, as well as other historical records.

Readers may find it useful to consult the glossary for fishery and Newfoundland words.

PART 1

CHAPTER ONE

Richard rushed into the kitchen with his bucket full of cranberries that had over-wintered, and then stopped dead. His mother was standing by the wood stove, her dark face pulled taut. The words she had just spoken still hung in the air. "He's only nine. He's too young to go fishing."

The wiry, stoical form of his father sat with his head firmly cocked to one side, a posture which Richard knew to mean he had made a decision and would not move. Both of them looked at Richard, his mother with a kind of desperate longing, his father opaquely.

Richard could almost feel his body splitting in two. To his mother he was the sharp student who liked school and would stay there as long as possible. To his father he was a shareman in the making, one who could not waste time idling at lessons of no practical use.

1

Richard put the bucket of berries on the floor. The sting of embarrassment hit his cheek like lightning and then rippled through his body. His mother lowered the dishcloth in her hand and silently let it come to rest on the table near her husband. She caught Richard's eye again almost with a hint of apology.

Over the next few days, Richard prepared for the change in his life. His father, Steve, was in the Banks fishery. The weeks-long voyages would be too much for nine-year-olds, even by Steve's standards, the Little Bay men joked. Thus, Richard was to go fishing with his grandfather Jim Hanrahan and his Uncle Michael in the shore fishery. That was their custom, to fish with brothers and uncles and fathers.

It was 1898 and Richard had spent his nine years of life surrounded by women and children. The men were more often than not away at sea; they were on the Grand Banks or on their way to the West Indies or Portugal or Spain, and sometimes to Greece and Italy. In Little Bay on the Burin Peninsula on Newfoundland's South Coast, the children played down near the salt water where they held contests to see who could skim stones the farthest, or in the thick evergreen woods where they dared each other to look for fairies as the warm summer evenings drew in. In the fall, their mothers gave them wooden pails and told them not to come back till they were full of blueberries. Picking berries was work but it was fun, too, especially watching the older girls and boys flirt with each other. Once in a while, Richard saw them sneak off in pairs to the deep woods, where no one would be able to find them.

"Well, we know what they're up to!" his sister Rachel would yell, forcing young couples to do about-faces, turning back into the openness of the barrens.

The boys made small wooden boats and sailed them in gullies or even in the harbour. They sewed bits of twine, fashioning little nets, in imitation of their fathers, who spent their winters mending cod traps. Once in a while they fought, even coming to blows over silly things.

Since Steve announced that his son would go fishing, Richard found himself standing aloof from these activities. It was as though he had been pulled by some invisible cord from his companions. He would never again sit in a school desk, he knew, and the thought of this caused him such grief he banished it as soon as it intruded into his consciousness. He felt as if he were just waiting now, though he didn't know for what. It was not as if he looked forward to going fishing.

*

During Steve's long absences, Richard had always marvelled at his mother, Elizabeth. She was a model of industry. Her abilities seemed to know no end. Everyday she made delicious bread from flour, water, and yeast, and on Sundays she added raisins if she had any and made tea buns. She made doughboys, too, and popped them in the meat and potatoes simmering on the wood stove. She grew the vegetables they ate: the plump potatoes, sweet carrots, tart onions, bitter cabbage, and juicy turnips. She worked capelin into the ground every summer to make the vegetables grow. Some of these crops she pickled and put in the long pantry at the back of the house her husband had built. She raised damson plums, too, and cherries and strawberries. From all these she made jams, putting them up every fall. Her ambition, Richard knew, was to grow apricots. If she didn't realize it, then she was confident her daughter Rachel would. "That girl is smart as a top," Richard often heard her say.

Like the other women in the harbour, Elizabeth made pies, but not too often because she had to "spare everything along" as she always said. The very phrase seemed to accompany the motion of kneading, chopping or scraping. She was a hunter, too. His mother went into the woods and onto the barrens, where she found rabbit trails and set small snares the way her father had taught her. She skinned the little animals and baked their dark meat, making gravy with their juices, and using their bones for soup.

She was a doctor as well, most often using the cherry tree as the source of her medicine. In the spring, she gathered trailing juniper from the hills along the coast and boiled it to make a tonic. "Drink it all down," she told her children. "It'll clean your blood right out." When they were run down and had boils, she made bread poultices that they held tight to their wounds. She burst blisters and stopped infections. She ground juniper for women to take as they struggled to give birth. She even made a cast from birchbark when one of Richard's cousins fell from a tree and broke his arm, with no other doctor around for many miles. She made sure Rachel and the other girls, Mary Jane and Annie, watched her and remembered what she did, so that they would be able to heal the ills of their own families someday.

CHAPTER TWO

At nine, Richard had about a year and a half of schooling altogether and was very smart, Elizabeth thought. He could read pretty well for a child with just a touch of learning. But she knew her husband had other plans for him, and she knew it was useless to argue. That afternoon when Steve told her he would send Richard fishing, she was upset but not surprised. He had been grumbling that the boy was always away with the fairies, always living in his head. And he was impatient that Richard couldn't fix on the task at hand, whether it was lugging barrels of flour up the hill to their house or spreading freshly caught capelin on their burgeoning vegetable patch.

Elizabeth was amazed how quickly Richard grew. Already he was a thickly set child with a pale face and square jaw. The pupils of his eyes were navy, rimmed with sky blue. Only his tendency to tan instead of burn hinted at the Micmac blood he inherited from her. Her girls, though – Rachel, Mary Jane, and Annie – they were "real Indians," with black braids down their backs and coal-black eyes. Their skin was burnt umber. They were like her own people from Piper's Hole River and Gallows Harbour way up in the bay. Richard, Elizabeth felt, was a Hanrahan, full of the Englishness of his Spencer ancestors from Marystown and England before that, and the Irishness of his forebears who had stolen into these coves and bays two and three generations ago, trading one form of harshness for another.

The Hanrahan men, who came long before any European women did, had married Micmac women, and maybe Beothuks, when they first over-wintered here. "There was only Indians here one time," the old people said. "This was the Indians' country." And that's why, Elizabeth thought, old Jim Hanrahan's face had the striking combination of sea-blue eyes and high, ruddy-brown cheekbones.

*

Richard fished near Beau Bois with his Uncle Michael, Steve's oldest brother, for a few years and with his grandfather Jim for one year. Jim had first fished in the 1820s. Beau Bois was where the Hanrahans fished, though no one seemed to know why or when they laid claim to the spot. Other families had other berths in the coves around Mortier Bay and on the way to Burin. Richard's stomach was delicate on the water, and he fought valiantly against the threat of seasickness which he felt constantly. The open air helped. So did the sight of land, somehow, or being able to fix his eyes on it anyhow. When the swell rose and he turned green, Jim put a piece of pork fat in his mouth. Almost instantly the boy threw up and felt immediate relief. Then he would be sick no more. In the first part of the fishing season he was throwing up almost every day. The men told him not to tell his mother; she would wonder why he wasn't growing. When he was thirteen and fourteen, Richard fished with his Uncle Dick, after whom his parents had named him, and some of his cousins.

The shore fishery was filled with cold early mornings, hand-lines and jiggers, dories bursting with slimy cod and the odd dog-fish, especially in the summer when the water was thick with them. His world was peopled by men as well as women now, and he saw how they needed each other. As a child, he'd only been on the beaches with the women as they'd made the fish; now he saw how the men slaved away on the water to get it.

*

During the months of the shore fishery, Elizabeth watched her oldest son roll wordlessly into bed each night. He would rise even before she would in the morning. He spent the winters in his uncle's fishing rooms repairing their cod traps. He turned ten, then eleven, and soon he had a hint of the stockiness of an ado-lescent.

But there was never very much time to think about it. Elizabeth worked in the shore fishery too and spent all her sum-mers on the beaches at Little Bay, Beau Bois, and Marystown, making fish with every other woman and girl in the bay who was old enough. Through the spring, summer, and fall months, the men and boys appeared in their dories, many of them from the Banks, others from the shore fishery. They hauled barrel after barrel onto the beaches. They dumped hundreds of pounds of fish in big piles on top of the rocks. Then Elizabeth and the other women started in on them. They washed the fish first in great vats of water, making sure that they were free of the salt they'd been preserved in at sea. Sometimes the boys helped with this task.

Elizabeth and the others uncurled each fish and flattened it completely so that it was splayed. They lightly salted them; this was the most important task of all, for the preservation of the fish depended on it. Then, with their long skirts rustling about their ankles, they bent down and laid them out, side by side by side till the beaches were obliterated by them. Sometimes they laid the fish on flakes, platforms made out of poles. They usually covered the flakes with tree branches so air could circulate around the fish. They worked fast, hoping the weather would not turn against them. Dry days with some sun and breeze offered ideal conditions for this work. Overcast days meant delays in curing fish, while rain was cruel, spoiling the fish.

In July and August the women sweated as they salted and spread the fish and rose up frequently to wipe their foreheads. The women tried their best to ignore the hunger pains that persisted in their bellies. They couldn't stop; they had to keep making the fish before the men dropped the next load at their feet.

Meanwhile, Elizabeth worried about Rachel's day back home, where the little girl baked and cooked for her brothers and sisters. On the beaches, the summer sun dried and cured the fish, thus making it ready for markets on the Iberian peninsula and in Jamaica. At the first sign of night, the women began stacking the drying fish in rows five feet high. These they covered in canvas to keep the night and morning dew away, until they could return to it after dawn. The women were not paid for their work.

The Doryman

As Elizabeth watched Richard work through the latter years of his childhood, she thought the sea was no place for anyone, really. In recent years, her people were more woodspeople. They had come to the Burin Peninsula from Bay d'Espoir, where they had been forced to retreat long ago when the island had been almost overrun by settlers. Then, later, they came back to the peninsula through the headlands of Fortune Bay to carry the mail overland. Only the Micmac knew the ancient paths and rivers between the South Coast and Trinity Bay and the Avalon Peninsula. They laid the telegraph cables, too, connecting one side of the island to the other with wires that meant news came faster than you could blink. It was awfully hard work in the wind and snow and ice, and solitary and dangerous. There were always repairs needing to be done. But they did the work because, like the settlers they now lived alongside, they knew little else.

*

When Richard turned fifteen, Steve decided to take him to the Banks. When she heard of her husband's decision, Elizabeth felt like one of the rabbits in her winter snares. She knew there was no sense arguing with her husband. He was a bit of a tough nut, they all said of him. Besides, he was that much older than her, which gave him even more authority than most men had. She was his second wife, too, so she never felt quite right in the marriage, even when they had loved each other long ago and she had left her home to come to his, as was expected of her.

*

It was mid-February when Steve and Richard set out on foot for Marystown. Earlier that week a cold front had moved into Mortier Bay, warning them of more wintry weather to come. Then

9

an Arctic Screamer had arrived from the northwest. Its strong cold winds pushed snow into drifts as high as houses and bent bodies nearly double as they walked into it.

Now the winds had died down, but the cold remained. The harbour in Little Bay was just about frozen over, so Steve and Richard copied across it, their small canvas bags holding a few possessions on their backs. It was a relief to get to the other side without getting their feet too wet. The air was frigid, so cold that the snow made scrunching noises with each step they took. The ruts in the path that led to Marystown were covered over with snow, but Steve and Richard walked along them as if they could see them. There were a few houses on this side of Little Bay, but not many, not like on the other side. Most of the homes over here were out on the Point, the bit of land that stretched into Mortier Bay. They climbed the hill out of the village and then went down the other side towards Marystown. Then the little dwellings petered out into nothing but a woods path that ran along the coast, and they began crossing Marystown and curving round to Mooring Cove. It was still several miles away.

As they walked along, Steve kept wiping his mustache with his hand, which was covered in the grey wool mittens that Elizabeth had made over Christmas. He was trying to get the ice crystals out of his beard. He said nothing. Although he'd never admit it, he was not looking forward to the days of slaving that awaited them. It'd be good for Richard, though, he told himself. It was time for him to get out from under his mother's skirts, which could not happen as long as the boy was engaged in the shore fishery.

Richard was silent, too. He kept himself occupied by thinking of the morning's events. That morning, Rachel had scurried into the room he shared with Jimmy and young Jack.

"I have a surprise for you, Richard," she said, her brown face all smiles. She pumped up and down on her tiptoes, making her almost as tall as her brother. Then she handed him a small package wrapped in brown paper.

He said nothing, but looked right at her. He was moved, but he didn't know what to say.

"Well, don't you want to open it?" Rachel asked impatiently, holding the package towards him. Oddly, he noticed how big her hands were.

"Come on, open it!" she cried.

Richard slowly took the parcel in his hands and gently pulled the string, loosening the paper around the small bundle. Then he sat on his bed and pulled out a pair of woollen gloves of brilliant white and hunter green. He turned them over in his hands.

"They're the colours of the woods in winter," Rachel announced. "And I made them for you, all by myself. I ev carded the wool. Mom's been showing me how."

She smiled with pride and her brother pulled her clo hug.

"Thank you, Rachel," he said. "I never even saw
them."

Now he smiled at the memory of his sister'
trudged alongside his father, the gloves keeping room

His mother, too, had tried to make his fi he was sit-
a little less nerve-racking.

One evening, when Steve was in U ng cotton shirts
down the hill, Elizabeth called her ol uite dim. She spent
ting in the corner chair near the wo
for her younger boys, though the

every evening this way, darning countless pairs of socks and putting new elbows in shirts and knees in pants. She made clothes from brin bags and dyes of blue, black, red and purple from berries and plant roots. Some nights she brought crazy patterns of colours together in the blankets and quilts that covered their beds and kept them warm at night. Sometimes she carded wool, sheared from the sheep she kept. Now she drew a scarlet ribbon bearing a medal out of her sewing bag.

"This is for you to take with you, Richard," she said. The medal twirled on the end of the ribbon, flirting with the light from the oil lamp. It was St. Anne, her hands clasped in prayer.

"It was blessed at St. Pierre on St. Anne's Day a long time ago, ᶜ⁻re you were born," she said. She smiled gently, and she + Richard's lips were clamped together. He was not one
on. Her own people were like that and, briefly,
ned so far away now, she recognized them in her
brushed his cheek with her long, dark fingers.
ᵗʰer and smiled shyly.
& out there," she said reassuringly. "St. Anne
but it round your neck and keep it on ... all

ly reached Mooring Cove, named after the
een moored there long ago. Then they
for one of the Brinton girls in Burin, on
was a proud forty tons, one of the
en this close. The glistening ice nee-
'e her look only more elegant.
anchors. She'll take in 2,000
much as 500 quintals more

12

than that," Steve announced, not expecting an answer from his son. "Not bad."

Richard's blue eyes scoured the vessel. Her hull was dark green with deep crimson rails and yellow trim. She was beautiful, no doubt about it.

"You'll get a one-quarter share," Steve said, patting Richard on the shoulder, "being a boy and first time out."

Then he looked down at his son and his face grew serious; there was even a hint of grimness. "I was fourteen when I started Banks fishing," he added, as if to comfort the boy. "Or maybe I was younger."

CHAPTER THREE

stle that first night, the men lay in their bunks and

f western boats and dories. They had kicked off

emoved the oilskins and sweater coats that

protection from the winter wind once they

recou...e captain and his mate slept aft in their own

Tim Wals...

from models, ...p woods near Winterland," Matty Dober

"She was a ...atbuilding. "Me and the brother-in-law,

And she was a model early last fall. We always built

We were was plumb...hard's benefit.

We were making the bo...g, apple-bowed and flat-bottomed.

He knows Tim is the bes...at's the way they are, these boats.

don't mind the woods myself...n Clarence Hollett over in Burin.

or making models. And I sure

ng on the water all summer."

He drew smoke from his cigarette.

"Captain Hollett used to buy his schooners in Essex in the Boston States. But in the later years, he wants to make them. 'Tis cheaper, I suppose."

"Yes, with we fellows pretty well indentured servants, I suppose it is!" said Steve. The men laughed grimly.

"Yes, there's after being thousands of schooners built in Newfoundland these late years especially," Matty said. "Before that, they used square-rigged ships and brigs."

"Schooners are ten times better, no matter which way you look at it," said Steve.

"Why, Father?" Richard asked, as he tried to imagine a brig.

"Lots of reasons," Larry Walsh from Beau Bois piped up. "For one, you need less hands with a schooner. The skipper's got to like that. More money for him!"

"Schooners can take the wind from either side, too," Steve explained. "And they're easier to sail in cold weather. Comes in handy in this country and on the Labrador."

"With the brigs you needed a hell of a lot of deck space for storing the sails and the rigging," Matty added. "So the jacks came in, the smaller schooners. And then the western boats came on and got real popular. That's what Captain Hollett wanted this winter, another western boat."

He began to describe them. "They have square sterns, son, the western boats, and the rudder is hung outdoors." Then he stopped. "Well, you've seen dozens of them."

Richard nodded – he had indeed seen dozens of the small schooners – and Matty continued. "We spent all October and November hauling wood and carrying it over to Burin.

Shipbuilding was always winter work. The Captain's son Philip, he's the master builder, takes after his mother's crowd from Fox Cove, I suppose. And then there was the painting, lots of painting." He paused for another draw on his smoke.

"Red copper bottoms and green hulls," Richard said enthusiastically. "And you had to tan the sails."

"That's right, son, that's a real job of work, sails are so heavy. Mainsails are hundreds of pounds."

He stopped again to emphasize the full import of the numbers.

"And then there's the dories," he continued, confident in his audience. "Captain Hollett used to buy his dories from Mr. Carter over in the Bay of Islands, Thomas Carter. The Captain always had double dories, of course. Thomas Carter started making them around '85. Before that the Captain brought them in from St. Pierre or up in the Boston States. The Lowells at Amesbury, they invented the dory, see? It wasn't invented in this country, though you might think it. We've been using them in the Banks fishery in this country for more than twenty years now."

Richard nodded.

"Simeon Lowell, that was the fellow's name," Steve added.

"That's right," Matty continued. "They started building boats more than a hundred years ago, in 1793, the Lowells, one generation after another. They charged one dollar a foot for each dory. So the average price would be fifteen dollars. They made them for the Portuguese and the French, besides the Americans, their own people, and the Canadians over in Nova Scotia. A lot of their dories were brought into this country, too. That stopped when the government here put a two-dollar tax on every dory you brought into Newfoundland."

"It was a good way to get dory-building started here," Steve said. Richard had never seen his father so talkative.

"Yes, true, true," Matty agreed. "Soon enough, Herder and Halleran started making them in St. John's. They had a factory on Hill O'Chips right near the harbour."

Richard imagined the crowds and noise of the city. He so desperately wanted to go there. His father had been there and to Halifax over in Canada. His uncles from Marystown had been even farther: to Spain and Portugal, and to hot countries in the West Indies, where they got rum and bananas. He wanted to see these places, too. He wanted to swelter in the heat like they did. Maybe this spring trip would be the start of all that.

"But Herder and Halleran's shop didn't last too long," Matty continued, obviously enjoying the fact that Richard was enthralled. "It burnt down in '91, when you were a baby, lad. They never rebuilt it."

"And the next year the whole damn city burnt down," roared Danny Spencer, who'd been quiet up till now. The men laughed at his tone. "Old Herder and Halleran were ahead of their time!" Danny added, to more laughter.

"Shouldn't laugh at other men's misery," Steve said sternly, rapidly changing the mood. Although Danny was a cousin, Steve thought him too frivolous and feared he'd be unreliable in a crisis. Danny sensed Steve's disapproval of him and, despite his sense of humour, tended to keep quiet around Steve.

"Well, they made fine dories, Herder and Halleran," said Matty. "They were fifteen and a half feet long and five-foot-four beam amidships. They used local pine, which is a nice wood.

17

I must say, I like Newfoundland pine. She's got a nice feel and is easy to work with."

The kerosene lamp flickered in the corner as the men talked of Monk boats from Monkstown up in Placentia Bay and of Harris boats. Gradually their talk grew more distant, and Richard found himself lying down and then drifting off. He dreamed of wide streets and houses piled on top of another and busy finger piers, rows of them, one after the other, as his father had described St. John's. There were horses and people everywhere, and shops, every kind of shop, most of them with candy in their windows.

"Put a blanket over him," Danny said.

"He'll be fine," Steve snorted. "If he's too cold to sleep, he'll wake up. We can't be babying him, I need him to work like any other man."

CHAPTER FOUR

"**G**et up and get to work!" a deep voice bellowed the morning after Richard's first night on the *Laura Claire*. It was 5:00 A.M. and still pitch-black. Richard tried to pull himself out of his sleepy state. He saw with some surprise that he still had his clothes on from the night before. At home he usually slept in a long nightshirt. Someone lit the kerosene lamp and Richard struggled to make out the faces before him. Everyone looked exhausted – they'd all walked long distances to get here – but the real work hadn't even started yet. The boy noted how grim they all seemed; the mood of the previous night had vanished as if it had never existed. The men were all business now. They quickly hauled on their clothes and jumped out of their bunks. Then they shoved their stockinged feet into their boots.

Richard smelled the strongness of toast right under his nose; the galley was right here in the forecastle. His face brightened at the thought of it as his eyes fixed on the cookstove in the cramped little space. Behind the cookstove was a hogshead that the men would fill with enough provisions for three weeks: salt pork, sacks of flour, oatmeal, dried beans, tea. The galley also held a water tank that they would fill to the brim.

But breakfast was an unceremonious affair on the *Laura Claire*. No one spoke as they grabbed cups of tea, barely taking time to drop sugar or milk into them. Then they took buttered slices of toast and ate them quickly, hauling their jackets on while they ate. Suddenly they all rose and dunked their dishes and cups in a pot of soapy water on the stove, giving them a cursory wash. They dried them and stacked them before hurriedly making their way through the hatch to the top deck. Richard followed, hoping someone would tell him what to do next, maybe his father.

But his father's thin frame was way ahead of him, and the boy himself trailed behind the last of the men, his relation, Danny Spencer, who was impatiently turning his foot in his boot to make it fit right.

On deck, Richard first saw Captain Brinton, a barrel-chested man with the dark beard the boy expected to see on a captain. The Captain nodded at each man as he emerged from down below. He even tipped his head toward Richard.

"This your boy, Steve?" he asked.

"Yes, sir," came the answer. For some reason, his father's tone made Richard feel something he had rarely felt before, something worse than embarrassment, deep in his belly. He couldn't quite pin a name on it, but he thought it was shame.

Then they all stood around the anchor chains, thick, heavy, ice-encased, and tangled on the deck.

"The sooner we get these sorted out, the sooner we can get on with the rest of it," the Captain announced.

As he walked away, the men lunged at the chains. *They're as heavy as Hero*, Richard thought, recalling the old horse his family kept back in Little Bay. He tried to figure how they could possibly untangle them. But the men had already begun chipping the ice off them, then lifting and turning them, grunting hard as they did so. Almost immediately, beads of sweat formed and then covered their foreheads, though it was freezing. Before long, Steve had removed his sweater coat; after an hour, Matty and Danny stripped down to their bare chests. So did Larry Walsh eventually. Sweat poured down their backs as they hauled more of the chain onto the deck. Somehow they managed to untangle it, link by heavy link.

Then some more chain appeared. Richard wondered if the anchor chain went all the way to the Grand Banks. He found the sight of his father labouring like this slightly painful, though he didn't understand why. He felt helpless; at his still boyish size, his efforts amounted to little. Good old Danny had figured out a way to make him useful, though; he got the boy to wipe seaweed and slub off the links to make them slightly less slippery.

At midday the men stopped work. Steve, Danny, and the other Catholics began the Angelus. In the grey cold, they raised their rote prayers to the Blessed Virgin Mary. By now, Richard's stomach was roaring with hunger, and he struggled mightily to concentrate on the prayers as his mother had taught him.

Dinner was pea soup, with not nearly as much ham as Elizabeth used in hers. There was hardtack, too, really hard tack. He feared he'd crack his teeth as he tried to soften it up in his mouth. He wished he was back home eating some of his mother's cooking, with Jack, Jimmy, and the girls at their long kitchen table. But then he admonished himself for being such a baby. What would the other men think if they could read his mind?

At this meal, too, the men ate in silence and in a hurry. They shoved their empty plates onto the counter and leaned back for a stretch. Then they collected their plates, washed, dried, and stacked them. No one asked for seconds. Then they grabbed hot mugs of tea and downed the liquid in a matter of seconds. At once, it was all over, and they rushed back up to the deck.

Back to the tangled chains. All afternoon they strained and sweated and grunted like animals as they pulled the links this way and that. Richard imagined he could see the flesh fall off his father's body, the man was working so hard. Steve was not a heavy man; he was tall and all sinew and muscle. No wonder, thought Richard, trying to guess how long his own puppy fat would last. Not long at this rate, he figured.

They worked as the sun went down over the peninsula and the darkness of the night descended rapidly upon them. The air turned frosty, and it was too cold to snow. Even as he sweated, Richard shivered. As the evening closed in, he began to grow dizzy.

Then someone, maybe Danny, shouted, "That's it! Six o'clock. Merchant's time is over."

"Thank God." Richard echoed one of his mother's favourite phrases as his bones screamed with exhaustion. He could sink into sleep so easily ...

"Come on, boy," his father said. "Time for supper. Then we've got to get to the trawls. The trawl tubs are waiting."

CHAPTER FIVE

Untangling the anchor chains took another couple of days of hauling, heaving, straining, and sweating. On the third day the sky grew bluish-grey, Steve looked up and said, "There'll be weather anytime now." He was right, for ice pellets began to rain on the men as they strained over the links of the anchor chains.

"It's too bloody early for hail," Danny said. "It's not April."

"It's not you who says what weather we gets," Steve answered, grim-faced and tilting his head skyward. Then he added, "That's it, that's all you can do. Best keep working."

Larry nodded, Danny sighed, and they all carried on. Richard paused for a minute to stare at the sky. The translucent spheres came down hard and fast, hitting the deck with little thuds. They bounced slightly, as if they were jolly and happy, putting him in mind of the small rubber balls his brothers Jack and Jimmy played with. Then he remembered that he was here to work, and he went back to the chains.

After their quick suppers, the men began preparing their tubs of trawl, the line with which the fish were caught. The *Laura Claire* carried five dories. Each dory required six tubs: four to be carried in dories to the Banks and two to spare. The trawls were 2,000 feet long, made of strong strands of tarred cotton. Every thirty-five inches or so another line, a ganger, was spliced into the trawl. The ganger was about thirty inches long and held a strong steel hook. Every trawl line had about 600 hooks. Until almost midnight the men repaired the trawls, replacing rusted hooks with new ones and inspecting every inch of every line.

The hardest work, after a day with the anchor chains, was stretching the main trawl to get the kinks out. Once again, the men strained and sweated, this time in the cold, dark night. Then they coiled the trawls again and placed them into the tubs.

"We're not allowed to do this during the day," Matty told Richard. "Not on the merchant's time, no sir."

"No?" the boy asked in disbelief.

"Uh-uh," Matty shook his head.

Richard didn't know it, but they would be at this work every night for the next three or four weeks. It was slow work that required some concentration in spite of its tediousness. It was dangerous work, too, and as the weeks passed, nips and cuts appeared on all the men's hands.

During the third week, when he could hardly see straight from work, Richard asked his father, "How much money have we made so far, Father?"

Steve snorted and then laughed from somewhere deep inside himself.

"Not one red cent," he said finally. "Nothing, absolutely nothing."

Richard was stunned. He could form no words.

"This is just preparation time," Matty elaborated. "We're just getting ready for the real work. We got to do all this so our gear is in working order to go fishing. Now *that's* the hard stuff."

Richard's mouth went dry and he tried to swallow. He thought of his mother and Rachel and wanted to go home, back to the shore fishery. Even further deep down, he wished he could be in school like his little brothers. But he couldn't. He was stuck on the spring trip, and he feared he'd be stuck on every spring trip for the rest of his life. He returned to the broken hook in his hands and, in his only expression of anger, ripped it off the trawl.

The crew of the *Laura Claire* gradually got through their daytime work, straightening out the anchor chains and then overhauling all the running gear, replacing what needed replacing. It was oily, smelly work, sometimes making Richard queasy. He was afraid he'd get seasick if the onshore smells affected him this much. Several times during shore fishing he'd nearly thrown up. Only the fresh open air had saved him. But he couldn't worry about that now. He had work to do, and plenty of it.

CHAPTER SIX

W hen the running gear was finally overhauled, the men began checking the standard rigging. By now Richard's arms were beginning to bulk up. Any excess fat was gone from them, and his little biceps were beginning to harden. He worked as hard as he could in his eagerness to please the other men. Once in a while the Captain strolled by to ask them how things were going. He rarely pitched in, and Richard saw how the men stiffened a little in his presence. Quiet anyway as they worked, they were always silent after he left. Again, Richard felt the red heat of a shame he could not articulate.

The men began replacing the broken ropes with new ones, and then they started the arduous task of removing the sails from the hold. This was no easy task, Richard was to learn. He had never seen sails folded up in ships' holds before. To him, they were always rigged, flapping, and pulling the western boats out of the harbour. It had never occurred to him that they weren't always attached to their masts, but he saw now that that was the case.

The sails were heavy, "damned heavy" as Danny Spencer said. This was especially true of the mainsail, which was seventy-five feet along the main boom and fifty-two feet along the gaff. It weighed 600 pounds, more than Matty, Steve, Danny, and Richard combined. So they tugged at it and heaved it slowly onto the deck under the bleak early-March sky. Again their faces grew wet with sweat, and they began the inevitable ritual of removing clothes to make their work bearable.

On the merchant's time, they brought up sail after sail and spread them on deck, ensuring that they were in good condition. They checked every inch of the hundreds there were, looking for frays and tears. Some of the sails had to be mended, so Steve and some of the others set to it with twine. As he sewed, Richard noticed that Steve squinted so that his eyes almost disappeared. *Maybe his eyesight is going*, the boy wondered. The next job was to hoist the sails: fore, jib and jumbo; midships, the foresail; and aft, the huge mainsail. This, too, taxed the men's strength, given the heaviness of the sails.

"It's important to get this job right, son," Matty said to Richard. "This is one real important job." The boy noted how the men seemed to take some pleasure in hoisting the sails, though it was still work on the merchant's time. He noticed that a small hint of anticipation crept into the air. The men seemed to feel that they were finally getting somewhere. In the evenings, though, they still scoffed their suppers like starving animals and worked on their trawls until midnight, frequently licking the blood off their fingers and pressing their thumbs into wounds to stop blood from flowing.

After some days, they were finished hoisting the sails. Captain Brinton stood on deck now admiring their work.

"All right," he said. "Tomorrow we sail to Burin. Should be a fine day for it."

The men all nodded. Burin was the headquarters of Brinton & Sons, the firm that owned the vessel. The Brintons were the Captain's family. It was the habit of South Coast Banks fishermen to bring the vessel to its owners and home port for the next phase of preparing for the spring trip.

The day itself dawned sunny and bright and the sky seemed to tease them with just a touch of spring. The Catholic men, who numbered more than half the crew, began the day with a decade of the Rosary down below. Even before they had eaten their breakfast, they said the first joyful mystery and envisioned the Angel Gabriel telling Mary that she would conceive and give birth to a son who would be revered by all the world. Their visions matched the anticipation that marked the day.

This was Richard's first time on a moving schooner, and his chest grew with the pride of it. He so wished Rachel and his mother and little brothers were here to see him off. He still missed them but was glad for the one Sunday he and his father had trekked out to Little Bay to visit them. They had been too tired on the other Sundays, when they spent the day laying in their bunks, listening to Danny's jokes and Matty's stories. Even during their day in Little Bay, they had both fallen asleep in their chairs as Elizabeth fretted about how thin Richard had gotten. And they had eaten like vultures in a desert.

The *Laura Claire* seemed equally proud as she left off her moorings in the cove. Her sails made thundering noises, so strong that the men had to shout to each other to be heard. To the south of them was Marystown, Creston North and Creston South, originally Christ's Town North and South, Matty reminded them. Mooring Cove itself had once been called Gold's Cove, a name which filled Richard's mind's eye with pirates and stolen loot. This was an old place for fishing. Men had come from the Basque country and France three centuries before Captain Brinton's schooner sailed out the bay that crisp March morning.

Mortier Bay, the massive bay that led away from the villages, was free of ice year-round. It was one the largest harbours in the world. In turn it led to Placentia Bay, Newfoundland's biggest bay. Placentia Bay was seventy-five kilometres wide at its mouth and had a depth of ninety-six kilometres, making it more than 3,600 square kilometres. For this reason it earned the title "that far greater bay" some years later.

Although Richard didn't know it – plucked from school as he was – English and Irish fishermen did not have access to Placentia Bay until the Treaty of Utrecht was signed by England and France in 1713. From that point on, the area was under British rule, and the French were no longer allowed to fish in Placentia Bay. Then it became the province of the English and Irish fishermen whose blood ran through his own, men and women who were transported from England or fleeing the poorhouse in Ireland, looking for a new life in a new world.

As they sailed out of Mortier Bay with Richard scrubbing the foredeck, the boy looked to the south and saw the mouth of Little Bay. He could not see the bottom of the harbour, for Little Bay was really a deep inlet, a fjord. All he could make out was the rich fir and balsam trees in the bottom. On either side of the narrow valley that made up the community were dots of houses. They looked so tiny from this vantage point, Richard thought, and unfamiliar in their smallness. He could hardly imagine the women and children inside them, going about their endless rounds of chores.

He could just about discern his family home atop a hill that rose some four hundred feet out of the water. He tried to picture his mother taking bread out of the oven and Jack and Jimmy and the little girls lining up for a slice, maybe with molasses if their mother had any left this time of year. He wondered if Rachel was standing on the hill, looking out for him, maybe waving. He looked around carefully and, seeing no one near him, waved slightly himself, just in case she was there. The gesture made him happy and he carried on scrubbing, satisfied with himself, his work, and the world. He would soon see Burin, the busiest town in the bay.

CHAPTER SEVEN

O nce the *Laura Claire* was outside Mortier Bay, the air grew colder. Back in the bay, the prevailing southwest wind had warmed the air, even this early in the year, and kept the perennial fog a few miles offshore. Here, though, the cold set in fiercely, and when the men were on deck, the dampness seemed to sink into the marrow of their bones.

The *Laura Claire* passed the mouth of Beau Bois Harbour and Duricle on her way to Burin. She sailed past little islands, some of them not more than rocks that rose up from the sea, clifftops, and harbour mouths. She streamed past larger islands, too.

Burin was the mercantile centre of the western side of Placentia Bay. The slipway here could accommodate the largest banking schooners in the fishery, vessels of 200 tons or more. Burin, or Burin Proper, as the people of Placentia Bay called it, was actually a collection of villages perched on bald rocks near the water. There was Pat's Cove, where a large extended family lived; Whale Cove, home to fifty souls; Shalloway, where over seventy people lived; and the much larger Step-a-side, named after the English town its first settlers had come from. There was also Dodding Head with only one family, and Great Burin Island, where more than 200 people lived. And Pardy's Island, home to another 170; Shandy Hall; Bull's Cove; and Narrows.

Many of the houses here were large: two, and even three-storied edifices with neatly painted trim, and grand picket fences out in front. Others, of course, were little more than shacks. And there were many in between. Unlike as in Little Bay, where everyone travelled on foot, there were horses and carriages here in Burin, and Richard felt giddy at the sight of them.

The streets of Burin were filled with people readying for the spring trip. There were coopers, sail-makers, shipwrights, and blacksmiths, all manner of tradesmen. There were cooks directing the loading of barrels of food – beans, pork, flour – onto the vessels. There were stores selling tightly woven cotton and even silk cloth brought back from more exotic climes than these. There was noise and lots of it: the clip-clop of horses' hooves, the smack of barrels on wharves, the shouts of the tradesmen, the laughter of small children, the call of their mothers.

The *Laura Claire* docked in Little Burin Harbour, between Bull's Cove and Path End. In awe of the place, Richard stood on the wharf and barely missed getting hit by a thick rope that flew through the cold air. Alongside the *Laura Claire* was the *Emma Jane* with her crew of Rushoon men, and the *Fair Haven*, crewed by men from farther up in the bay, places like Southeast Bight and Petite Fort, not too far from where Richard's mother was from, though he'd never been there. Steve and the others seemed to know most of the men from deep in the bay. The men of the *Laura Claire* all doffed their caps to Captain Moulton and Captain Travis as they walked ashore. As the captains passed by on their way to the Brinton offices, Richard found himself looking at the ground. That uncomfortable feeling invaded his pores again and his cheeks flushed red.

"Two hundred years ago, the French fleet hid in these harbours," Matty said, interrupting the boy's thoughts. "They were hiding from the English, see? They hid on little islands and coves tucked away like this one. Sir John Norris commanded the English and he was after them. I guess he was a bit of a terror."

"Yeah?" Richard replied, somehow sounding much less interested than he really was.

But Matty didn't need the boy's affirmation and continued. "And not too long after that, Captain Cook was here, Captain James Cook."

"I heard tell of him," Richard said excitedly. "He's right famous."

"Indeed he is, lad," Matty nodded. "He surveyed the whole of the Burin Peninsula. Sure, that's where Cook's Lookout got its name." He flicked his head in the direction of the lookout.

"Oh!" Richard said. It had never occurred to him before that real things happened here, in this place near where he was born. In the irregular schooling he'd had, he'd heard only a little about the English kings and queens and battles fought and bloodshed way over in Europe. It thrilled him that such a figure as Captain Cook had been so near the place he knew as home his entire life.

"Captain Cook was all over Newfoundland, sure. There was privateers here, too, lad," Matty said, widening his eyes. "Sure, they were here less than a century ago, in your great-grandfather's time when they first came over from Ireland. Burin had to have fortifications, sure, there were so many privateers."

"Privateers? Really?" Richard said.

"Yes, son," Matty answered, nodding studiously. "They were from America, and they were hard old men. Tough and greedy, nothing could stop them. These were dangerous waters one time, my boy."

Suddenly, Burin seemed to offer all manner of adventure to Richard. But he found there was not much time to explore the town. In fact, there was virtually no time. The next stage of preparation for the spring trip began almost the moment they docked. Again, their hours were filled with non-stop work. As soon as the *Laura Claire* was moored, the men traipsed up to the Brinton premises where their dories lay in storage. They fetched their small boats, five in total, and lugged them down bottom-up to a cleared space on the wharf near their schooner. Richard watched his father's eyes go over his dory, Dory Number 2, with a fine-tooth comb, taking in every detail. He took the oars in his hardened hands and turned them over again and again, like a surgeon examining his patient. Some minutes passed. He turned the dory over and peered into her belly. Then with his son's help he lowered the dory into the harbour and floated her to check for leaks. They hauled the dory up and Steve examined her once more. When he was done, he patted the little boat twice on the upturned bow.

"She's all right for another year," he said, almost happily. Richard smiled. Things seemed to be going well so far.

He watched his father take some thick rope and make nose straps and stern straps for the dory. Then his father knotted them into place, his hands doing a frenetic dance. He then set about on making repairs to the oars, which showed some battering from the previous season.

Like his shipmates alongside him, Steve checked his dory's thwarts again and looked more carefully at the bulkhead, which he removed from the dory and noted was a little worn. "It'll have to be replaced," he decided. "It's best to take no chances."

The next day his father showed Richard how to make a bulkhead. They used no pencil or paper; instead, Steve did all the calculations in his head. They retrieved panel wood from Brinton & Sons just up the hill and cut the wood to the right size and shape. With some help from the other men, they inserted it in the dory. It fit perfectly.

"She's seaworthy now," Steve announced finally. Richard noted that his father seemed really to be in his element here in Burin, in the middle of all the frantic activity that marked the beginning of the year's Banks fishery, and in spite of the cold that still seeped into their bones. Things here were so different from the matriarchy that was Little Bay and the quiet that characterized their days at home.

With the dories in good repair, the men walked up to the Brinton & Sons stores again to get paint. Every dory heading out to the Banks had to have a fresh coat of paint. That was their tradition, and they took pride in it. Their carpentry finished, the men set about carefully applying paint to the little crafts. They all used yellow, paler than lemon but with a nice glow, as was the practice.

Then they began hauling chocks aboard; these were large puncheons they retrieved from the store sheds. They needed six large puncheons for each boat to make into liver butts, where the Captain would render the miserable-tasting cod liver oil. They also dragged on board four large fish crates where they would cut, throat, and head the fish they caught. Then they made two large fish tubs by sawing a puncheon in two. These were for washing the dressed fish.

Still on the merchant's time, the men checked the splitting tables and stored their trawl tubs and bait jacks. Then it was time to build the gurry kids on deck; these were large wooden boxes or pounds in which fish offal or "gurry" would be stowed.

At night they scarfed their suppers as usual, washed, dried, and stacked their dishes, and made the last repairs to their bait hooks. At this stage there was a little time for rest, and they all knew they would need it when they got to the Banks.

But first, another dreaded job had to be done. The *Laura Claire* needed salt, lots of salt to preserve the fish. The men braced their bodies as they loaded 250 hogsheads of salt onto the schooner. They split into three groups to do this in the most efficient manner possible. The first group was stationed in the Brinton fishing rooms where they shovelled the salt into the wheelbarrows. The salt was heavy, much more than the heaviest snow, and seemed to be in unlimited supply. The second group, of which Richard was part, wheeled the salt on board the schooner. They used a bridge of planks the men had made at the crack of dawn. Pushing the wheelbarrow up the planks and onto the boat was the most difficult part, and more than one man rushed forward to help Richard with it, though never his father. The third group of men stood on deck; in their calloused hands were shovels which they used to throw the salt into the pounds in the hold. Their backs strained as they did this and, again, the sweat poured off them. They ignored pulled muscles and kept working all day. It was still the merchant's time.

CHAPTER EIGHT

One morning Captain Brinton called Richard to the bridge. The Captain patted his chest, a habit he'd carried over from his asthmatic childhood, as the boy walked in slowly, tentatively. Clearly Richard was frightened to death of the Skipper, which, of course, Brinton easily recognized. He knew that the boy must surely fear being summoned by the Captain. No doubt he was afraid he'd be sent back home for some infraction that only the Skipper had noticed. Brinton surveyed the clothes stretched tight on the boy's growing body – he was covered in a sweater coat that seemed to be shrinking – and saw the paleness of his face. He tried to set the lad at ease.

"How old are you, son?" he asked in a low voice, trying to sound gentle.

"Fifteen, sir," Richard answered, staring at the deck.

"Fifteen," the Captain repeated, thinking the boy looked barely into his teens. He paused. "Well, I suppose that's an all right age for a boy to start Banks fishing. And your father is with you."

"Yes, sir," Richard said, still eyeing the deck.

"Relax, lad," the Captain said. "I hope it's going well for you."

"Yes, sir," said Richard.

"Good, then," Brinton answered. "Will you run up to the store for me and get this order? It's my personal order. I need tobacco and such for the spring trip. It's all written here." He pulled a note from his breast pocket and glanced over it. "Can you read, young Hanrahan?"

"Yes, sir, a little, I mean, I ..." Richard's tongue seemed to be thick and unmoving.

"That's good, very good," the Captain interrupted, trying to rescue the lad from the despair that was evident on his face. God, the boy would have to toughen up a little. "Anyway, the shop-keeper can read and so can the serving girls, so you'll have no trouble."

Richard stood in his place.

"Well, be on with you, then," the Captain said. "Off you go."

Richard clutched the note in his right fist. Here at last was a chance to see some of Burin in daylight all by himself. The store was at the far end of Bull's Cove, and Richard made his way along the ruts in the road. The snow that had covered them most of the winter had melted from the heat of the abundant traffic. *It'll take awhile for the snow to melt at home*, Richard thought, there being such little traffic. Along the way, he passed two ladies with great feathered hats on their heads. Were the hats heavy? he wondered. He had never seen such high, fancy hats; in Little Bay, the women only wore bonnets. So pretty these were here. He tried to picture his mother in such a hat, but quickly decided it would not suit her. And where would she wear it?

One horse and rider after another went by him in both directions. Most of the horses were dark as the night. Only a few had thick legs and hooves like Hero back home. Richard realized that he was alone now, although he was surrounded by people and their noisy activity. No one was telling him how to push the wheelbarrow or paint the trim on a dory. The sternness that radiated from his father was left down there on the wharf while he was up here in the town. For the first time in many weeks, he felt the busy feeling in his head cease. He relished the feeling and settled into a relaxing stroll to the store.

Finally he reached it. It was in a large, flat-roofed building next to one of the grandest houses in Burin. The house, painted white like most in the town, had rows of windows and a fence that surrounded it. Richard's eyes settled on it. Then he walked up the steps to the store, slowly, taking it all in. He noticed the white letters on the window. He tried to read them: *so-ap*, what's that? *Ladies' dresses*. He recognized that one. Wouldn't it be something if he could save enough to buy his mother a dress? And maybe dresses for his little sisters? They would be so happy, and his mother could have a rest for a few evenings instead of blinding herself with needles and thread. *Hats*, that was an easy one: his surname started with "H". *Wash-buckets*, he figured that one out. Same with *molasses*, and *rice*. But *S-ho-es*, he didn't know what that was. Darn, he wished he'd had more schooling. His heart cried out for the little classroom that had cocooned him those few winters, but that he'd left behind long ago, forever.

His thoughts were broken by a voice that sounded harsh at first. "Who are you?" it said. "What are you doing?"

Richard looked away from the window to see a blond boy, a head taller than himself. The boy was dressed in dark overalls and wore a clean heavy jacket over them. On his head was a work cap of the kind Richard had seen the tradesmen wear.

"I'm Richard," he answered, wondering for the second time that day if he was in trouble.

"Oh, Richard who? And where are you from?" the bigger boy asked, his brow creased in seriousness.

"Hanrahan, from Little Bay," Richard said.

"Oh. Good afternoon. I'm Peter, Peter Moulton from Salt Pond, but I live here in the harbour now." His features softened, and Richard relaxed with the knowledge that the boy was merely curious. He nodded.

"What're you doing here then?" Peter asked.

"Fishing, well, getting ready for the spring trip," Richard said, feeling a little surge of pride. "My father and I are on the *Laura Claire*. She's that big schooner down there." He pointed to the dockside, where the activity looked like it was being carried out by little dolls far away.

"Hmmm. Aren't you too young for that, though? You're not very big. How old are you?" Peter asked.

"Fifteen, I turned fifteen on Christmas Eve," Richard said. "I was born in 1888. How old are you?"

"You don't look that old. I'm sixteen," said Peter. "And you haven't asked me what I do here, but I'm going to assume you're wondering and tell you anyway." He paused and stared at Richard. "Well, I'm a shipwright."

"A shipwright?" Richard repeated, not quite sure what Peter meant.

"Yes, well, I'm learning to be a shipwright," Peter answered. "I'm an apprentice. I work with my uncles over there." His arm flew in the direction of two large wooden buildings down by the water.

"Matty and Tim on our crew make boats in the winter," Richard said, thinking of his fellow crew members. "That's winter work, building boats. Do you fish, too? Are you going on the spring trip?"

"No," Peter shook his head. "I work here year-round. Lots of us stay ashore. The coopers, the sailmakers, blacksmiths, and tinsmiths. We never go out to the Banks. Or to the shore fishery, either. We stay here ashore."

Richard could not fathom a man or boy who did not go to sea. He looked quizzically at Peter, scarcely believing what his ears were telling him. None of the men in Little Bay stayed ashore, not unless they were on their deathbeds.

"Boatbuilding is winter work for some men," Peter continued. "For fellows who do the odd bit of building: dories and western boats. And lots of those fellows go to the Banks come spring. But for us, shipbuilding is year-round work." His chest puffed up proudly. "Mostly we build schooners. We use models to start. I know how to pick the wood and saw the planking and frame for small schooners already. I can easily build a dory."

As Richard's blue eyes stared up at him unblinking, he continued. "Lots and lots of schooners are being built in this country now. Hundreds of them, no, thousands. Schooners are the thing now. They'll be in Newfoundland forever."

"I helped my father build a bulkhead for our double dory last week," Richard ventured. "I liked doing it, it was good work."

Peter nodded.

"I like shore work," Richard added.

"Yes," Peter said. "And that's only a small job, building a bulkhead for a dory. Imagine what it's like building schooners all the year round." His eyes widened, and Richard nodded solemnly. Did he dare hope he could get work like this someday? Some of the men had said he was good at carpentry, a real quick learner, they'd said.

"Uh oh," Richard said, suddenly remembering why he was here on the steps of the store. "I've got to go. I've got to get things for the Captain. Tobacco and such. I better hurry. I'll see you again, Peter."

Peter tipped his cap in Richard's direction as the boy rushed into the store.

*

In the forecastle at night, Richard heard stories that he thought would scare the life out of him. He had grown up hearing of shipwrecks and drowned fishermen, but never had these tales seemed so real. He had seen his long-faced father and uncles bury the victims of storms and gales, but it never occurred to him how dangerous the Banks fishery really was. This was rapidly changing now as he lay in the hold of the *Laura Claire*.

CHAPTER NINE

There were literally thousands of shipwrecks off Newfoundland. A century before Richard went on his first trip to the Banks, one in eight of the ships that left Bristol heading for Newfoundland never made it. It's likely that they were lost, not near England but on the western side of the Atlantic, because the western side of an ocean is always the roughest. Since then, in the last forty years of the nineteenth century, more than 2,000 men died in almost 100 shipwrecks near Cape Race on Newfoundland's southeastern tip. Thousands of fishing vessels had been lost there and elsewhere on the island, including hundreds of schooners which were the hope and pride of the whole bay and the rest of the South Coast.

Ships sank and lives were lost because there were no weather forecasts, or because those weather forecasts they did have were inadequate. Predicting weather for the island, where the cold

Labrador Current clashes with the warm Gulf Stream, was much more of an art than a science, and notoriously difficult to do. Sometimes weather forecasts were rendered useless by sudden storms that no one expected, strong currents that defied study, and high winds and seas that daunted even the most experienced captains and mates. Often the winds carried rain, drizzle, and dense fog that reduced visibility at sea to almost nothing. Sometimes these storms escalated to August Gales, the demons that haunted the South Coast and its people. These gales were the violent aftermaths of hurricanes from the faraway south. They would often take the lives of fishermen.

Many schooner captains did not have good navigational aids. Magnetic compasses and sounding leads were all subject to error. Few captains had chronometers which could establish longitude and latitude; these were too expensive.

Sometimes, in the winds and the fog, vessels hit sunkers, large rocks lying in the water that easily tore ships to bits. Human error, too, brought on by fatigue, inexperience, or fear, also contributed to the shocking death toll. Every year on the South Coast the numbers of widows and orphans grew, but the men still fished. This was Newfoundland, and they had no choice if they were to eat and live.

The South Coast fishermen went right out to the Grand Banks, more than 150 miles off the southeast tip of the island. Famous as the world's richest fishing grounds, the Grand Banks had a depth of between twenty-five and ninety-five fathoms and were 36,000 square miles. They were a vast expanse of dangerous, grey waters and black sky. The Outer Bank, or Flemish Cap as some called it, is a continuation of the Grand Banks, extending even farther into the Atlantic Ocean. The Flemish Cap was as deep as 160 fathoms. The cod lived here: huge steak cod, bigger than some men, and with spines that seemed made of steel. And cod was Newfoundland currency. These were not the only Banks, though. There were many more, totalling 75,000 square miles – the size of a respectable country on some continents. There was St. Pierre Bank, Green Bank, Whale Bank, and Mizzen Bank. The South Coast schooner fishermen knew these places like they knew the lay of the little rooms in their homes. They knew Banquereau, first named by the Basques, and the Virgin Rocks, where so many vessels were lost. Farther west, they fished off Burgeo Bank and Rose Blanche Bank. There was also Brown's Bank, LaHavre Bank, christened by the French, and many more. And there was Cape St. Mary's, the jewel in the crown. "Cape St. Mary's pays for all" was what the Placentia Bay fishermen reassuringly told each other.

Nations had fought over these Banks and the rich fish harvests they yielded as long as memory went and beyond. France, Spain, Portugal, England, Canada, America, Newfoundland, all these places had laid claim to the Banks on Newfoundland's doorstep. Shots had been fired and wars initiated. Cod was King and everyone wanted a part of it.

CHAPTER TEN

The men of the *Laura Claire* ended their shore work in Burin. The water tank behind the cookstove was filled and the hogshead in the galley loaded with provisions. The dories were in good repair; the trawls, tubs, and tables ready for what lay ahead. The men had been at it for well over a month and hadn't earned one cent in all that time, as Steve had told his shocked son some weeks before. They weren't paid anything for the preparation work. In fact, they often went into debt during this time. They needed new bait hooks from the merchants and new trawls, sometimes even new tubs for their trawls. They needed paint, too, for the dories, and rubber boots and oilskins and sou'westers, the hats they wore. All this added up and was marked against the money they would earn on the Banks. They usually bought from the same merchant who owned the schooner or western boat they were on.

47

Actually, they wouldn't earn any money at all. No coins or bills would be placed in their hands when the trip ended or the season was over. Instead, they were paid in kind, given by the merchant goods to the value of the total their fish was worth: sugar, flour, Kingfisher boots, tea, maybe some cloth. The numbers were the merchant's, and not all merchants were benevolent. The dorymen didn't question them.

All over the island, this system ruled their lives and was called the truck system. Rarely were Steve and the others ever out of debt. Some years they might crawl a little closer to the zero line on their accounts, but more often than not they sank further into debt, and they got just enough goods to get them through the winter until the spring trip. Sometimes they didn't get that much. It depended on the price of fish, and its quality. There were winters when they knew what it was to scrape the bottom of the flour barrel. There wasn't much satisfaction in this side of their lives. It was full of fear and worry. At these times they were thankful for the bounty of the land and sea, which kept hunger at bay; it offered them everything from dandelion greens to partridge to rich, dark seal meat and clams that they dug from the shore.

This trip the *Laura Claire* headed to St. Pierre Bank, not far from the only remaining land in North America over which France had control. As they sailed south past Chapeau Rouge – "Red Hat," the French dubbed it – Richard watched the land and saw that its form kept changing. The voyage out was the only time the dorymen could relax, though Steve always found something to do, even if it was just scrubbing out the forecastle again.

"That's the way of Chapeau Rouge," Steve remarked as he joined his son at the railing. He was silent for a minute, and all they could hear was the constant chop-chop of the waves. Then he said suddenly, "Better get back to work now. Captain won't like dawdling. This ain't a holiday."

*

Richard's heart pounded as he and his father rowed their dory away from the schooner before dawn two days later. It was strange being on the water like this, even before the first light of day. It gave him an eerie feeling. And a lonely one. It was as if the rest of the world had disappeared and they were floating even farther away from it.

At two-thirty that morning, Captain Brinton had taken soundings and dropped anchor. Then, at his command, the men had begun baiting up under a kerosene lamp attached to the mainsail. In the hold, which took up most of the belly of the schooner, they shovelled herring into baskets. Then they brought the baskets on deck, where they unloaded the herring and chopped it roughly with bait knives, trying not to get cut. Then they baited their hooks quickly in the cold black of the night. Richard's lips were chapped, but he hardly noticed this as he gobbled his breakfast of fish chowder after two hours of baiting.

They had hurriedly unstacked the dories and put the thwarts and bulkheads back in. Still rushing, they fixed kerosene lamps to the gunwales of each dory. In each little boat they put two tubs of baited trawl, two light kedge anchors and buoys, a large, two-pronged fork for pitching fish, an extra barrel of bait, a breadbox with a bit of grub in it, and an earthenware jug of fresh water for the inevitable thirst they would feel in the dark salt air. Their aim was to get as much fishing in as they could before nightfall and the dangers it brought.

Now, in the early dawn, his stomach churned as it had when they'd left Burin. Sometimes the food inside seemed to jump up into his chest, but he always managed to swallow it. He felt dizzy, too, and had to work hard to focus his eyes at times. In the bunk at night, it was as if his body were spinning like a top; in fact, the image of his little brother Jimmy spinning a top never left his head. It was seasickness, he reasoned, had to be. But he wouldn't dare let on, not to anyone. He didn't know what his father would say. Or the Captain. None of the other men seemed ill, and he didn't want to let anyone down. So he suffered through it and somehow managed to keep his grub inside. He didn't know that throwing up would bring at least some relief for a time. No one had told him this and he didn't ask.

Richard thought, and hoped, his sickness might disappear when he was in Dory Number 2 with his father. It was a smaller boat with no funny smells, and they'd be in the bracing fresh air. It wouldn't be unlike the shore fishery, he told himself.

But now he recalled that even off Beau Bois, a small boat was pretty sheltered, not like here on the open sea. And Little Bay was doubly sheltered. He'd never been out in storms or even rough weather, which he considered this to be, though it seemed not to faze his father. There was no denying he was a sufferer of sea-sickness. Did it ever get better? Did it go away? Was there anything for it? he wondered.

As the schooner disappeared into the damp fog that was characteristic of the St. Pierre Bank, he grew frightened in the little dory. What would happen to them if a storm came up or a sudden tidal wave carried them away? He'd heard of tidal waves around here, and everyone knew there was no telling when a storm would erupt. Just how far from the ship were they? It seemed as if they had been rowing forever. In spite of the open air, Richard still felt queasy and his arms ached from rowing. His father's impatience with him was making him feel worse. Steve was like a rider pushing his horse to the limit. Richard was too tired and sick to realize that such slaving was his father's only insurance against a hungry belly.

Then they stopped rowing. Or, rather, Steve did, saying nothing, and Richard quit rowing, too. He hoped against hope that they'd have a little break now, maybe eat a bit of hardtack. As difficult as it was to get it down, hardtack was the only thing that his belly could tolerate.

But no, the next phase of work started immediately, as Steve set out their first line and tied the dory to the buoy at the far end of the trawl lines. There was a little rest, finally though Richard could scarcely enjoy it as he rocked helplessly in the boat, fighting a rising queasiness. Steve looked at his son suspiciously but said nothing. Instead he lit a cigarette and smoked it, the wisps of smoke adding to the cocktail of smells and sensations threatening Richard's stability.

Then, suddenly, they began to underrun their trawls. They pulled up the line – the work giving Richard a welcome respite from thoughts of his plight – with Steve in the bow gaffing the fish off the hooks. Richard noted the cruelty of his father's actions, of any fisherman's actions, including his own, but he dismissed it and rebaited the hooks. Then he dropped the line back into the inky sea to wait for more fish.

Steve counted every shiny wet fish that appeared in their little boat.

"Count them yourself," he ordered Richard. "Every fish. Never trust the skipper or anyone else to count them for you. You just don't know."

Richard had learned that they would be paid by the fish, specifically the number of fish they caught. It didn't matter then to the fishermen if they caught small fish or huge ones; weight didn't matter, only numbers did.

Some five hours later they rowed back to the schooner. The dories had left the *Laura Claire* like the spokes of a wheel, going outward away from her and each other. Now they returned in balletic fashion.

Richard wondered how one dory's lines could get entangled in another with a system like this. He knew this happened, but he couldn't see how. He was afraid to ask, though. Besides, he didn't really care; he was feeling unwell again. He was cold, and his stomach refused to settle down. Out of the corner of his eye he noticed blood trickled down his father's right hand, but the older man ignored it and rowed as if his life depended on it.

Richard and Steve used pitchforks to unload the slimy, silvery cod from the dory onto the schooner. It was hard work. In the four fish crates they cut, throated and headed the fish, working as rapidly as they could. On the splitting tables, they quickly removed the backbones using square-topped knives with curved blades. In the two fish tubs they washed the dressed fish. Still hurrying all the while, they loaded it into the holds to be salted.

They threw gurry into the gurry kids, the large wooden pounds they'd built back in Burin, on deck.

"You can't dump gurry on the fishing grounds," Steve said curtly to Richard, his hands bloody as he flung fish guts to the container. "It'd be bad for the water and the fish." Richard nodded, grateful whenever his father spoke to him like he was just one of the men, but still feeling queasy.

Finally the Captain joined them in their work. He stood over the liver butt into which the men threw dozens, then hundreds, of cod livers of all sizes. Richard watched Captain Brinton take a fryer, a stove-like contraption with a grate and a fan-shaped funnel, and put it through a square hole in the top of the first butt. He heated the fryer with dry kindling and soft coal at first. Then he added hard coal after a while. When the oil was rendered out of the cod livers, the Skipper removed the fryer and placed it in the next butt to begin the process over again. There were four altogether.

"So that's how they make that rotten stuff," Richard said to himself. He could taste the horrible oil in his mouth, remembering his mother's insistence that all her children swallow it every day in winter. The memory made his stomach begin flipping and flopping again.

When all their fish was finally salted, Steve jumped back into his dory and Richard followed him. Again they rowed out to the fishing grounds, again not saying a word, and again they fished and returned to the *Laura Claire*, where they gutted and salted their fish. They did this twice more that first day.

That night Richard was so exhausted even his stomach pains and spinning head could not keep him awake. For the first time since leaving Burin, he slept soundly.

CHAPTER ELEVEN

One day was like the next in the Banks fishery. The men's hours became an endless round of rowing, baiting hooks, letting out trawl, hauling trawl, unhooking fish, counting fish, pitching fish onto the schooner, heading them, gutting them, tossing their livers and guts, throwing them into the hold, salting them, rowing, fishing. The only variation came from their meals, which the cook tried his best to make satisfying, and the dreams that filled their few hours of sleep each night. Through it all, Richard tried his best to ignore the queasiness that never left him and sometimes threatened to overwhelm him.

By the fourth day of fishing Richard was throwing up uncontrollably. He hadn't eaten much the whole trip because of his sickness, so before long he vomited green bile, which cut his throat with its bitterness. Then convulsive dry heaves overtook him. His eyes were bloodshot from the fruitless effort of throwing up. Tiny pinpricks of red appeared on his pale cheeks, put there by the force of his retching. As the men rose from their bunks in the morning dark, Richard found he could hardly stand up.

The men gathered around him after breakfast, the very smell of which made him retch even more. They said little but looked at him intently, trying to figure out if he was seized by seasickness or something even worse.

"Have some hardtack," Matty suggested. "It's good for what ails you."

"You'll be able to hold it down," Larry Walsh added. "That's the thing for seasickness."

Richard slowly shook his lolling head as he leaned against the bulkhead of the galley.

"Drink something," said Danny, sounding worried for once. "You got to have water in you or you'll get the dry heaves."

Richard nodded, meaning he already had the dry heaves, but the men misunderstood. One of them shoved a mug of water into his face. Richard licked his dry, cracked lips and stuck his tongue into the mug. He tried to drink a little. But he immediately began vomiting again and he couldn't stop himself. He sprayed drops of water and the bile that remained in his stomach all over the bulkhead and the floor underneath it.

Richard was almost too sick to feel embarrassment, but his face grew red and hot anyway in some sort of primitive, almost automatic response. No one said anything. One of the men backed into the galley to get a rag cloth and bucket.

"He's awful sick, that boy," Matty said finally.

"There's no time for sickness here," Steve said gruffly. "And there's nothing wrong with him that can't be cured."

Without warning, he leaned his right arm back, then pulled it forward and hit the left side of Richard's head. Then the right. Then the left again. And the right. The thuds echoed in the boy's head, and he winced from the pain and the dizziness that enveloped him. But Steve went on boxing his son's ears till the boy almost blacked out.

"Give the lad a break, Steve, b'y," Danny said sternly.

"He's fifteen years of age, for God's sake," someone else added.

"And he won't be seasick anymore, I guarantee it," Steve answered. He looked at his son on the floor now, shivering slightly and trying to hold in his whimpers. "Now get up and get to work," he barked.

Somehow Richard rose slowly from the floor, his head feeling as fragile as an eggshell. He said nothing. He couldn't have spoken if he wanted to. He tried to focus his eyes on the steps in front of him. He ignored the men who still stood standing around him. Then he followed his father up top and to Number 2 Dory, where they would spend most of their day.

The air was cold and wet with drizzle and fog. It was hard to see beyond the schooner. Richard pulled his oilskins close to his body and got into the dory. His head was filled with pain and his stomach ached. Even worse, he felt an excruciating combination of shame and fear. But gradually he became frozen, all of him, his mind, his body, his heart. And, despite everything, he was able to carry on. Somehow he didn't feel as seasick as he had since the *Laura Claire* hauled out of the harbour.

Though the weather was miserable, the fishing that day was easier. There was a fish on almost every hook. For once, neither of them cut their fingers. Richard's seasickness levelled off to a manageable state and he tried to forget about the morning's events.

As they rowed back to the schooner, Richard watched his father out of the corner of his eye. His mother, he knew, would be disgusted with what her husband had done to his son. But she'd probably be afraid to say too much. Instead, she would treat her son to lassie bread and talk quietly to him as he got into bed. She'd treat him like he was her little boy even though he was almost a man. There was no sense trying to say anything to Old Steve. Here on the St. Pierre Bank, Richard's life back in Little Bay seemed so far away now. Now Richard wondered: Was his father cruel? Was he mad? Was he human? Was he possessed by a demon or something? Did he know it hurt like hell to have your head beaten in?

Richard looked at Steve's uneven lips, sternly pressed together. He took in the sunken eyes, the long, thin hands, and the tightness of his father's body as he imagined it through the oilskins. He saw the baldness of the older man's head, the remaining hairs turned grey and white, and the crevices that were worn deep into his narrow face. The boy realized that he could not recall ever seeing his father smile. He watched the frantic way Steve rowed. It was the same frantic way he did everything. His intensity never wavered, onshore and at sea. He was not yet forty.

How old did Steve say he was when his own father first took him out here? Fourteen? No, younger maybe? Did his father box his ears, too? Did anyone say, "Don't be so hard on him, he's just a boy"? Richard saw the constant fear of starvation in his father's eyes. No, he didn't think they did say those things.

Richard didn't feel anger or hatred towards his father. He felt only fatigue. And a hardness in his chest that had not been there before.

Around them were low grey clouds and choppy dark waves. They were in the middle of a mizzling rain, marked by drizzle and a thick mist that seeped into the bones. There were no blackbacks or hagdowns sailing through the air. They could see no other dory. The water made the only sound, and it sounded angry.

Richard pushed his teenaged body into his large wooden oar and helped haul the dory back to the schooner.

CHAPTER TWELVE

Finally, Captain Brinton decreed that it was time to return to port. When Matty told him this, Richard was so relieved he let out air that he did not know he had been holding in. He hated it here in the middle of the cold ocean, the middle of nowhere, a godawful place where they did nothing but suffer from back-breaking work and bone-deep fatigue. He was sick of all of it: the hardtack, the salt beef that was parcelled out to them, the fish soup that they gulped down every evening. He had never experienced life as so fruitless and gloomy. He felt like a bear in the woods that does nothing but search for food. There was no joy, no happiness, never any laughter. Out here, there was only the trepidation he felt in the presence of his father and the Captain, worry about how many fish they were catching, and fear of the weather that could turn at any moment and take their lives.

Richard tried to take pride in his work – he knew that's what his mother would tell him to do – but somehow he couldn't always do this. There was too much fatigue in his heart and in his young body. Sometimes, although he would never tell his mother, there was even hatred, for the water, for his father, for the Captain and the damned Banks fishery.

He thought of these things as the *Laura Claire* headed around Chapeau Rouge. "Red hat," he remembered Steve said it was called in French. He thought of the ladies on the streets of Burin, the ladies with the fancy hats with feathers coming out the top. Then he thought of his own mother and her big strong hands. *She will never wear a fancy hat*, he thought.

He knew, too, that he wouldn't be able to buy nice dresses from a store for his sisters. It had gradually dawned on him as the men talked and tried to joke about it that he'd never see money this trip. Nor any other trip this year. Maybe never. Instead, all his slaving might help erase a little of his father's debt, built up through two and a half decades in the Banks fishery. That's all his hard work would do, all it could do. It'd mean they'd have tea, some flour, and a bit of sugar, that's all. It'd keep them alive, but not prosperous, nor enjoying the rewards of their labour.

He remembered setting out that February day from Little Bay to Mooring Cove with his father. He recalled the anticipation he'd felt, in spite of the fear, and even the hopes he'd dared to feel. He laughed an old man's laugh as the keenness of his disappointment took hold. Things were the way they were and there was nothing he could do about it.

The *Laura Claire's* first stop was Burin, where the Brinton family's enterprises were headquartered. Back through the passage of islands they sailed, their hold bursting with fish salted down. Back to the berth between Path End and Bull's Cove. Once again, the streets of the busiest town in the bay filled Richard's eyes and teased him with dreams. They would stay here a couple of days, to be spent unloading fish. Then they'd move into Mortier Bay, where they'd bring fish to the women who waited in Beau Bois, Little Bay, Creston, Marystown, and Mooring Cove.

During their first day ashore, Richard managed to get away from the *Laura Claire* and the fish-covered wharf alongside her. He felt the unsteadiness of his legs. Sea legs, they were called. It took him awhile to walk completely upright and straight without any difficulty. Many of the men landing here walked like this, so many that the harbour seemed full of drunks.

On the wharf he struggled to get his footing. Eventually he walked steadily, and then with the step of a man. He looked not at the muddy spring ground but all around him at the carpenters carrying lumber, the fishermen pushing wheelbarrows full of dead fish, the horses clip-clopping by, the sheep that scrambled up the hills that ringed the harbour. His toes were curled under in the boots that had become too small for him, but as he walked, he held his head high.

It didn't occur to him that Steve might be looking for him, that his father wouldn't approve of him taking half an hour to take himself off on a walk. He couldn't worry about such things now. He wasn't afraid of his father anymore. He was just desperate to have a few minutes to himself.

At the top of one of the hills, he saw a familiar blond head out of the corner of his eye. Yes, there he was, there was Peter Moulton crossing the path that led from one of the largest white buildings in the harbour to the other. Even at this distance, Peter seemed taller. His increased height made the confidence with which he walked even more noticeable. Richard watched him silently.

He thought of Peter's life, working ashore with his uncles the whole year round. Even in summer. He imagined the work the young man did, shaping from beautiful wood the boats in which the men of the South Coast would spend their lives fishing. Peter, he knew, would never be paralyzed with seasickness and have his ears boxed by his father as a cure. He'd never have to lick the blood off his hands on a cold, lonely offshore bank.

When he had met Peter weeks ago, Richard had wondered if he could do work like him, work that was filled with craftsmanship and comfort. He smiled at the thought of this, but his smile was rueful, even bitter. He knew now that such work could never be his. Fishing on the St. Pierre Bank, hauling the heavy wet trawls into the dory and ripping the fish off the hooks had told him somehow. He had learned his place in the world, he knew where his destiny lay – on a cold, wet sea in a dory – and he knew in his marrow he had no choice but to accept it. As he thought of this, something inside his body twisted. He would never even voice his wish to do the work of an onshore tradesman. He had learned not to, so he kept it to himself from that day on.

CHAPTER THIRTEEN

The *Laura Claire* pulled into the mouth of Mortier Bay after sailing all day. Her crew were happy to leave the cold, wet air of St. Pierre Bank behind them. It was warmer here in this little micro-climate, and they noticed the edge of comparative dryness in the April air.

As the schooner moved into the bay, Richard looked over and smiled, thinking how he would finally see his mother before the day was out. His hands were calloused and hard now, but his wrists were covered in water pups, blisters, that refused to heal. They'd been put there by the chafing of his oilskin sleeves against his skin. Were they ever tender! Worst of all, they sent pain right through him whenever he used his hands, to lift food to his mouth, to haul the last of the trawls back into the tubs, to pull a line, to cut the head off a codfish. There was no relief.

"You get used to those water pups," Matty had said.

Richard doubted it.

He was pleased for at least one thing. His seasickness had almost completely disappeared. All the men were surprised by this, except, apparently, Steve, who said nothing whenever they spoke of it and marvelled at it. He would only look into the distance, his gaze directed at something far off.

Richard was relieved to no end. But he also felt a kernel of anger that it took a beating from his father to cure it. Now as they headed into Mortier Bay, he looked over at his father and saw again the deep curves that radiated out from the corners of his eyes, and the downward lines of his lips. His mother raised him with stories of Indians spearing eels in shallow pools in the darkness of the night, and walking deep into the woods to hunt bear and render the grease that was so special to them. The comforting feel of her soft body would always stay with him, as would the sound of her gentle voice. He felt happy, even loved, in her company. His father, though, had given him no stories. He realized that he hardly knew Steve, a man who seemed to spend most of his time in his own thoughts and said little.

Before Richard knew it, the Captain had dropped anchor. They were outside Little Bay, and Richard could easily make out his family's small white house on top of the hill on the east side of the fjord. On the shore he saw figures in long skirts that blew up like balloons in the wind; they had seen the schooner and were waiting! His heart jumped a beat at the thought of his mother standing there waiting for him. *Maybe Rachel will be there, too,* he hoped. They'd both be proud of him, he knew, and his little brothers would be in awe of him. They'd see him as a man now, he reckoned. It was a nice thought that gave his heart comfort.

The Doryman

The men lowered Dory Number 2 into the deep waters of the
bay. This was Richard's cue to join his father in the little boat.
Next they set down Dory Number 4, from which Larry Walsh
and Val Kilfoy fished. They were going back home to Little Bay,
too.

The deck was full of activity now as the men pitched salt fish
out of the dark hold and into the dories below. The fish kept
coming and coming. The Captain counted them, and when he saw
Steve's thin lips move silently, Richard knew his father was
counting, too. "Never trust the skipper or anyone else," he had
said firmly so many times as they'd fished in the fog.

Finally their dory was bulging with fish and the pitching
stopped. Up to their hips in fish, Steve and Richard rowed
towards their village, stroke by stroke. As they neared the shore,
they jumped out of their boat and strained to pull it onto the
beach.

*

Richard was in his mother's arms. "Oh, darling," she said
again and again as she hugged him tight, ignoring his wet, bulky
oilskins. "You're all grown up." Her eyes were darker than he'd
remembered – they were almost black – though it had only been
weeks, and she'd swept her long hair under her bonnet. Her skirt,
wet at the hems, reached the rocks on the beach.

Then Rachel, lanky in a cousin's hand-me-downs, rushed up to
the pair of them and pulled them apart so she could see her
brother.

"You've grown taller," she announced to the entire harbour.
Then she opened her brother's jacket and sized up his chest and
legs. "But you're awful skinny!" she added.

"Get to work now," Steve interrupted, ending the reunion that Richard had conjured up so many times as he rowed back and forth to St. Pierre Bank. The women moved back and the men began filling wheelbarrows with salted fish; these had been fetched by the local boys. Steve, Richard, and the other men pushed the wheelbarrows over the beach rocks to their premises. Then they stacked the fish in tidy rows in their fishing rooms. It was too early in the year for the women to make fish – to lay it flat on the beaches where it could dry and cure in the sun. April drizzle and fog created a dampness that seeped into everything. So the fish would stay in storage until June.

His water pups aching – his mother hadn't noticed them during their brief meeting – Richard got back into Dory Number 2 with his father and rowed back out to the *Laura Claire*. The schooner's deck was awash in codfish, and when the dories reached the ship, the men rapidly filled them to the thwarts with it again.

After Richard dumped his last load of fish, his mother came over to him. "Go on up to the house," she said quietly but firmly. He could see that she had planned to say this for some time, but Richard hesitated; he wasn't sure if he should go back to the schooner. That's what his father seemed to be doing. He didn't want to defy his father, or displease the Captain. But he wanted to go home and see his younger brothers and sisters. He knew they'd be impressed with him.

"Go on with you," Elizabeth said, pressing the palm of his hand between her long calloused fingers. "Run on up now." She nodded, urging him on.

So he did. His oilskins streaming behind him, he lunged forward in the direction of his home at the top of the hill. He ran and ran as fast as he could, leaving the *Laura Claire*, the drying fish, Dory Number 2, and his father far behind. As he neared the top of the hill, his jacket fell off and he left it there behind him in the late spring slush. He continued running, hard and fast. He was surprised to find his eyes filling with tears. He let out a dry, deep, solitary sob as he ran into the April wind and neared his home. But he didn't know why he was crying, for never had he felt so free.

PART 2

CHAPTER FOURTEEN

Oderin was once the most important island in the bay. Lying in the western part of Placentia Bay, it was only one and a half square miles, fashioned like a horseshoe. Its open end looked to the southwest and offered ships welcome shelter against the gales that haunted the bay each year, especially in August.

It was named in the 1660s, after Audierne, a small port in Brittany, France. Oderin had a central place in the history of Newfoundland's South Coast and appeared very early on in the historical record. The first people to winter over on the island were two Frenchmen in 1704, Ricord and LaFosse, men whose first names are lost to time. LaFosse came with his family; he was on the run from the French, who had accused him of spying for the English. Everyone who lived on Oderin knew that he had buried treasure down on the beach, in a tunnel between Beach

Pond and Castle Island. The old people said LaFosse's ghost haunted the tunnel, and they had no wish at all to see him.

The rise of Oderin as a centre of commerce began when Christopher Spurrier, a merchant from Poole in England, set up a fishing and shipbuilding enterprise there in 1773, on the north side of the harbour. An ambitious man with his sights set on the growing South Coast fishery, Spurrier set up premises in Burin and other spots at the same time. He sent some of his 150 fishing servants stationed at Oderin to Baine Harbour, Boat Harbour, and Rushoon on the Burin Peninsula to cut timber, for there was very little on the island.

The people who came to Oderin from then on were mostly English: the Baileys, the Butlers, Drakes, Smiths, and Mannings. They had winter houses on the Burin Peninsula where they could better access wood and hunt rabbits and partridge from December through to March. Eventually some of them began to stay on the peninsula year-round, but others returned to prosecute the summer fishery from Oderin. Then Spurrier descended into bankruptcy. Injecting a bit of glamour into Oderin life, local rumour had it that Spurrier's wife frittered his fortune away at the gaming tables in England.

Spurrier's place was taken by an Irish-born merchant called James Furlong, who set up shop with another man called Hamilton. Irish settlers followed Furlong to the island: the Murphys, Powers, and Clarkes, people who had had enough of being itinerant or tenant farmers for English landlords, others who'd been driven off the land, a few in search of adventure.

Late in the nineteenth century, a young Mr. Edward P. Morris, the brother of the local priest, came to Oderin to take up his first teaching position. Later, he would become prime minister of Newfoundland, something in which the island people would take pride.

Politics was not new to Oderin, though. Richard McGrath was elected the Member of the House of Assembly for Placentia and St. Mary's Bays in 1861. More than twenty years later, his son James F. was elected to the position. Oderin became the hub of the bay and certainly its most important island. The way officer was stationed at Oderin, so that letters might be sent and received. So was the police constable, and the customs officer. Early in the twentieth century, Dr. McCullough came to the island; he was the only doctor on the Placentia Bay islands.

In those days, the sea was a highway and Oderin was one of its main stops. Every fall, huge shipments of fishing gear – nets, dories, navigation equipment for schooners – came in from the St. John's firms of Job and Bowrings, who bought the island's renowned fish. Men carried crates of supplies from ships to wharves and fishing premises: tea, molasses, sugar, pork, and flour. Local schooners went to Prince Edward Island in Canada to buy beef and farm produce that they sold all along the South Coast, stopping first in Oderin where they knew there was a good market for it. Spirits, tobacco, and rubber boots were brought in from St. Pierre. Gear for the five lobster factories on the island was landed. This was a prosperous place.

At the centre of Oderin society was Lady Day, the annual devotion to the Blessed Virgin Mary and garden party held in August. On the morning of Lady Day, the harbours of Oderin were chockablock with dories, western boats, and tern schooners. People came from all over the bay, whether they were Catholic,

Church of England, or Methodist, to celebrate and see each other in the middle of the summer fishery. There was food, games, and dancing, and for a young woman, the chance to meet the man who would become her husband.

CHAPTER FIFTEEN

Angela Manning was a native of Oderin, the great grand-daughter of William Manning who had come to the little island from Bristol, England with his wife Margaret in the early 1800s. She had just returned to Newfoundland from New York, where she had worked as a maid for four years. She wanted to see something of the world before she settled down and got married back home, as she always knew she would and as she wanted to. Lots of the young women from Oderin were going into service in New York and Boston then. They used the connections their fishermen brothers and uncles had from fishing out of Gloucester, Massachusetts to get good situations. It was more exciting than going to St. John's, as so many of the unmarried women of the South Coast did.

In New York, Angela worked for the Spurrells who lived in a Brooklyn brownstone. They were a family of English descent whose father had spent some time in Newfoundland with a fishing enterprise in Trinity Bay. The Spurrells still had relatives "back home" as they called it, even those who had never lived there.

Angela's day was cluttered with work. She rose long before dawn to start the fires in the kitchen and drawing room, where Mrs. Spurrell would start her needlework right after breakfast. Her next task was to help the cook, a black woman called Rosa. The cook was elderly now and had been born a slave in Georgia. She had been in service her whole life and had never married.

Angela took the bread from the breadbox – white, they never ate brown – and cut enough slices for Mr. and Mrs. Spurrell and their four children, Lillie, Andrew, Evelyn, and George. Then she got the oats off the top shelf in the pantry and laid out the butter, sugar, tea and milk for Rosa to prepare breakfast. She buttered some bread for herself and gulped some of the tea that Rosa made for the two of them. Then she crept into the bedrooms and collected the chamber pots, which she then dumped outside. She cleaned them out before replacing them, fresh for the first use of the morning.

By now, the younger children had awakened. Angela went into the boys' room and fetched baby George's clothes from the wardrobe. Then she went into the girls' room and chose a dress for little Evelyn. She went back to George then and dressed him. When she was done, she returned to Evelyn and helped the little girl, who was into her petticoats by then. Lillie and Andrew were old enough to dress themselves.

Rosa set the table, between stirring the oatmeal and making the toast, but Angela always cleared it and brought the cutlery, cups, and dishes back into the kitchen. As Mrs. Spurrell settled into the drawing room, Angela always remembered to ask her if she was comfortable with the fire. Angela had figured out early on that it was best to have the mistress of the house as an ally, should anything go wrong. Like most girls on the Placentia Bay islands, she had only three years of schooling; her mother had plucked her out of the classroom to help with the younger children. But Angela's brain worked non-stop, and she was described proudly by her parents in Oderin as "smart as you can get." She was more than a competent reader, and in the top drawer of her bureau she kept a notebook into which she copied prayers and her favourite poems.

After Mrs. Spurrell was settled away, and the two littlest children by her side in the drawing room, Angela got Mr. Spurrell's briefcase from his study and put it out by the door so he could take it as he left for work. He was an accountant for an import-export firm, who took the subway into Midtown Manhattan every day. He never spoke to Angela, only nodded in her direction once in a while. That's for the best, Angela often reflected, all too aware of the pinching, teasing, and worse, much worse, that other young women in service had to contend with.

Then Angela walked Lillie and Andrew to school a half-mile away, answering Lillie's incessant questions about everything under the sun on the way. Although the Spurrells seemed to Angela to be well off, both children attended Public School 30 in central Brooklyn, rather than a private academy. She wondered if this was a philosophical decision, or whether the Spurrells conserved their funds in case providence decided to deal them a financial blow someday. After all, their roots were in Newfoundland, where few people took the future for granted.

After the children were ensconced in school, Angela walked back to the house, where a mountain of chores awaited her. She made the seven beds in the home, swept the three layers of floors, beat the area rugs, fetched wood from the basement, stoked the fires, washed windows and walls, dusted in every room, mopped the porch and hallway floors, and did laundry.

Washing clothes was the hardest and most time-consuming task of all. Angela started by gathering the dirty clothes from the three bedrooms upstairs. She stripped sheets and pillow cases off the beds and tore down any curtains that needed a wash. Then she took the clothes to the basement – sometimes this took two trips from the top floor – and sorted the fabrics by type and colour. She went upstairs again and boiled water on the stove upstairs in a large pot. When the first pot was boiled, she carried it downstairs and put another on the boil. Downstairs, she poured the water into a steel tub, added lye soap – store-bought, not like back home where they made their own soap – and soaked the clothes. After a time she ran upstairs to check on the boiling water, which she carried downstairs, and took the soaking clothes out of the tub. Then she put the washboard in a washtub with clean water, loaded the clothes in, and started scrubbing. It took her the better part of the morning, because she always had more than one load, and she had to start the process with each load. By the end, her arms were sore and her hands chapped.

She fed George and Evelyn their lunch at midday. Rosa had laid it all out. It was usually tomato sandwiches with vegetable soup, though sometimes the children had pea soup or chicken sandwiches. Angela brought Mrs. Spurrell her lunch in the drawing room. Angela ate her lunch, which was whatever the children were having, on the run. She cleared the table and then brought George and Evelyn upstairs for their nap. Evelyn hated her nap and usually refused to go to sleep. She cried and tried to cajole Angela into letting her stay up, but Angela was firm and took no nonsense.

With the children finally asleep, Angela went into the kitchen and got the shopping list from Rosa. It was the younger woman's job to go to the butcher's, three-quarters of a mile away, and get the meat. Some days it was flank steak, others it was ham. Occasionally fish was on the menu, and Angela always took careful note of the quality of the fishmonger's offerings. Walking to the butcher's or fishmonger's was the most enjoyable part of Angela's day. She had no children hauling on her skirts and no one telling her what to do. She was alone with her thoughts. Sometimes she thought of Oderin and her parents and brothers and sisters. Other days she merely enjoyed the Brooklyn street sights: the crowds, the endless rows of brick houses, the buggies, even the odd car. She loved to pause over the flower stalls and smell flowers she had never seen before. Most days the butcher, young, dark-eyed Giovanni Casanelli, flirted with her. "I hava the besta meata for you, Mizz Angela," he said to the tiny, blue-eyed woman. And "Are you sura you are notta Italian?" But Angela laughed out loud and did her business; she had no real time for New Yorkers because she had her heart set on going back home.

She dropped her purchases at the Spurrells' and then went to fetch the children from school. When she got home, she got George and Evelyn up from their naps and helped the other children change out of their school uniforms. The rest of her afternoon was often filled with washing either windows, floors, or clothes. She heated up the iron and pressed the clothes at this time as well: Mr. Spurrell's white shirts, his wife's blouses, and the children's uniforms. She put the clothes and sheets away. When Mr. Spurrell came home at six-thirty, she helped Rosa serve supper to the whole family.

After clearing away the cutlery and dishes, Angela sat down with Rosa for her own meal in the kitchen. The two servants talked about their work and the family's comings and goings. On a rare occasion, Rosa would tell Angela about life on the Georgia plantation where she was born and reared. It fascinated Angela; she could not believe that one person could own another, no matter what colour they were, at least until President Lincoln changed the law and there was a war. The men in her family knew what it was like to do unpaid work, though, and she told Rosa that. The older woman's big eyes grew even wider. "Imagine, white folks doing work and not getting paid for it," she said, shaking her head and laughing. Angela joked with her that she should come to Newfoundland and see it for herself.

After their bit of fun, it was back to work for both women. Angela stayed in the kitchen while Rosa washed the dishes, and she began work on a pile of clothing that needed mending. They were quiet as they concentrated on their work. Angela's work was usually interrupted by Mrs. Spurrell's announcement that it was time to bathe the children. After their bath, Angela got their nightclothes and helped the little ones change into them. She said good night to the children but didn't tuck them in; that was their mother's job. As the night closed in, Angela tackled one more load of wash, hers and Rosa's. She rarely got through the pile that awaited her. She was tired by this time, so every night the pile seemed to stay the same size. She didn't worry about it, though. Worrying was not her way. Do your best, she told herself, that's all you can do.

In the meantime, she looked forward to the one Sunday she had off every month. On those rare days she slept in until eight o'clock, went to nine o'clock Mass, and had a nap until her dinner with Rosa at noon. Then she read a few poems from her notebook and took the subway into Manhattan to spend the afternoon exploring the largest – and finest, to her mind – city in the world.

CHAPTER SIXTEEN

In his twenties now, Richard Hanrahan was fishing with the Mannings of Oderin. Captain Paddy Manning owned a western boat that was headed for the Virgin Rocks in 1912. On board was his son, John, who became fast friends with Richard, and his younger son, Tom, as well as sundry crewmen from Oderin and Baine Harbour on the Burin Peninsula. A six-mile run from the island, this was where Paddy's wife's people came from. There were ten of them altogether in addition to the cook, a cousin of theirs from Oderin.

Richard was finished fishing with his father. They'd been to the Grand Banks, the Virgin Rocks, Whale Bank, Mizzen Bank, and Burgeo Bank. One year, they'd worked together on a small boat in the shore fishery. It allowed them to sleep in their own beds at night, but there was even less financial reward in it than in the Banks fishery. Afterwards, Richard went looking for another schooner to take him on for the spring trip. The Holletts of Burin took him up, and he was off again to the Banks. Steve had stayed out of the Banks fishery that year. He started work as the ferryman in Little Bay, taking people from one side of the fjord to the other in the punt that he rowed. It wasn't nearly as hard work as fishing on the Banks, but like the shore fishery, it brought in less reward. Still, he wasn't getting any younger; his arms were wracked with arthritis and his knees were stiffer all the time. The family could afford to have him acting as ferryman as long as Richard and young Jimmy and Jack went to the Banks. He had taken Jimmy out there a couple of years after Richard's first spring trip, then Jack. Thankfully, the younger boys hadn't gotten seasick, and, like their brother, they were quick learners. All of them were hard workers, and as far as Steve was concerned, that was the main thing.

Steve was slowing down in other ways, too, and he'd taken to drinking whenever he could. Elizabeth hated it. He got even more ornery than usual, and sometimes he got angry. It was no example to set for the youngsters, she thought, and even the young ones were old enough to notice what was going on. Was this what he wanted for them?

He didn't drink every night, as he couldn't get his hands on liquor that often. But he went to St. Pierre three and four times a year with a bunch of fellows from over in Marystown to get rum. They brought fish and wood to the St. Pierre people, who lived on a bald rock in the middle of a fogbank. In return, they got barrels of rum that they hid in caves on the boot of the Burin Peninsula. When they wanted to go on a tear themselves or had a customer for some of their stock, they rowed out to their hiding places and retrieved their booze.

Elizabeth knew St. Pierre as the place her people went to be baptized and married in the old days. It was a holy place, where the priests lived. How things had changed.

Steve would sit in his kitchen while Elizabeth and his daughters cooked and baked around him, trying their best to ignore his ranting. He talked incoherently about the time his dory got lost on Green Bank, about how the merchants took advantage of him every year, how he worked harder than any doryman in this bay, yet he could never get ahead. Now, why was that, he cried. Why the hell couldn't he get rich, or even out of debt for once? It was damned unfair, it was.

Once in a while, Steve plunked down in the kitchen with his rum bottle and drank quietly, but not often. During those times, he called Elizabeth over, and when she approached him he grabbed her and held her tight. "My pretty thing," he said, still sitting and burying his head into her bosom, ignoring her acute embarrassment in front of the children. Then he started crying, sobbing even. "Stop it now," Elizabeth said. "What's wrong with you? Don't be doing that in front of the children." But he ignored her and kept on crying. Slowly, Rachel, Jack, and the others crept out of the room and quietly went upstairs, leaving their mother alone with their drunken, tormented father. None of them ever spoke about it, not even to each other.

Richard had witnessed a couple of these incidents. The first time, he stared at his father and grew angry as he watched his mother squirm, red-faced, and looking helpless. Then he broke in between the two of them and told his father to stop. "That's enough," he said, sounding more tentative than he'd meant to. His heart sank at this. He wanted his mother to know he was on her side.

"You! Get lost," Steve answered angrily, his eyes narrowing, his mood changing in a flash. "I'll say what I want." He sneered at his son in a challenge.

Richard pulled his mother away and stood between the two of them. He said nothing, but his defiance was there for all to see. His brothers and sisters watched in silence. They were scared, afraid of the threat of violence that flooded their home. But Steve's inebriated attempt to pull himself out of his chair failed. He could not rise, he was too drunk.

"That's enough now, Richard," Elizabeth said finally.

"Aaagh," Steve muttered as he waved his hand in dismissal of his ungrateful wife and son. *Who cares about them anyway,* he thought and took another swig of rum. Then he went into himself and stayed there until he passed out.

The second time Richard saw his father sobbing into Elizabeth's breast, he stormed out of the kitchen and then out of their house. He was mad at his father for his crudeness and rough ways, but he was fed up with the way his mother put up with him, too. *Why doesn't she give him a good kick,* he wondered. Then he thought of Rachel and her incessant chatter about how she was going into service in St. John's and how she'd have such adventures in the city they couldn't possibly imagine. The lot of them drove him mad sometimes. Suddenly a trip to the Banks looked good, especially without the ferryman.

CHAPTER SEVENTEEN

By now, Richard was an old hand at the Banks fishery. He had done all manner of work. The Newfoundland Banks fishermen gutted, dressed, and salted their own fish as their vessels did not hire men for these purposes, unlike the boats out of Nova Scotia and Gloucester, Massachusetts.

He had grown accustomed to tragedy and trauma. One year he had gone to the Grand Banks with a Burin Peninsula crew, among them a father and son from Spanish Room. The two men had left their schooner in Dory Number 3 in late spring weather that was foggy but mild. They didn't return to their vessel. The Captain waited, pacing the deck and hoisting his flag to show other schooners that he was missing a dory. A long, dark night passed with the two men out there somewhere on the water. The fog was still thick the next morning. When it finally lifted, all hands were hopeful the Spanish Room men would return.

But they never did. Their bodies were never found, nor was their dory. The older man left a widow and several children still living at home; his son was to be married that summer. Such events were all too common amongst Banks fishermen.

Another year, one of his fellow crewmen, a young man from Fox Cove, drowned in an accident that could have happened only in the Banks fishery. Again it was foggy, blindingly so, and the schooner ran into the man's dory, causing it to capsize. He was thrown into the cold ocean and, like many fishermen, could not swim. He panicked, and swallowed a great deal of frigid sea water before anyone could get to him. That was his captain's last voyage; indeed, he spent the rest of his shore days a recluse.

Not all captains were so sensitive. The dorymen spoke of skippers who kept on sailing when men were swept overboard. They were lost to the waves and cold water anyway, they reasoned, so few of them could swim. They'd only be going back for bodies, and that was a waste of time. They were in a rush to get back to port so they could unload and get the fish to market.

Captain Paddy Manning took on Richard Hanrahan as a doryman every spring now. He liked the young man's work ethic. Richard went at a job with a vengeance until it was done. He never complained, not even when others did. He took the initiative, too. He spotted things that needed doing and did them before he was asked. And he was a top-quality salter. He was getting a reputation as a salter all over the coast. He was a good example for the Captain's younger sons, Tom and the other boys from Oderin.

Sometimes, though, Captain Paddy wondered about Richard's studious ways. He had something of the scholar about him, although Paddy had never seen him read. There would never be such an occasion, of course, with the life they led. He was awfully serious. He seemed rarely to smile. He seemed a bit driven, as if there were a force of unhappiness behind him, pushing him along. Paddy wondered if Richard knew how to enjoy himself. Yet he knew the young man was a good one. He hoped that the years would be good to him and that the stiffness in his back would give way a little.

On Lady Day, the harbours in Oderin were blocked with vessels of every size and shape. They came from Gallows Harbour, Baine Harbour, Petite Forte, Monkstown, Burin, Spanish Room, Marystown, Little Bay, Lawn, and the Banks themselves. They came from Long Harbour, Red Island, Merasheen, Fox Harbour, Harbour Buffett, St. Bride's, Argentia, and St. Pierre. Anglicans and Catholics came to celebrate the day. Even some Methodists appeared. Very little of the religious conflict that marked life on Newfoundland's northeast coast reared its ugly head here. Protestants and Catholics ate and drank together. Some, like Richard's grandmother Rachel Spencer, a Protestant, and grandfather Jim Hanrahan, a Catholic, even married each other.

As he made his way across a crowded meadow with his mate, John Manning, a cup of tea in his hand, Richard first saw Angela. She had just returned from New York, and she carried with her an air of urban sophistication, most apparent in the mauve feathered hat that sat on her head. Richard's eyes rested on it, and his mind drifted back to the first time he saw such hats in Burin long ago, just before his first spring trip. God, that was so long ago and he had thought those hats were so beautiful.

She was so pretty.

"How do you do?" The voice was loud.

"Dick? Dick? " John was speaking to him.

"Sorry. Oh, sorry! I was just ... How do you do?" He nodded and took her hand. Her eyes were sky-blue, and her name was Angela, which reminded him of angels. She was laughing because of their exchange, but there was no mockery in her laughter, just the hint of camaraderie. She was full of fun, there in her purple hat. He offered to get her some lemonade, and she accepted. John smiled and ever so quietly drifted away from them. He had seen something in his sister's eyes and knew that it included only Richard and herself.

The day after Lady Day, Richard, John, Captain Paddy Manning, and the rest of the crew of the *Bridget*, named after the Captain's wife, sailed to the Virgin Rocks in search of cod. The breezes were gentle, the clouds high, and the sun warming and pleasant. The summer air infused them with a lightness they rarely felt as they scrubbed decks, mended sails, baited their hooks, loaded their trawl tubs, and then rowed away from their western boat when they finally reached the Bank.

Captain Paddy enjoyed the days, too, but he kept an eye on the sky and the water. "It's August," he said every so often. "August Gales, you know."

Their habit was to fish as much as they could, to stay on the Bank until their vessel was loaded. One day towards the end of their trip was particularly hot. John and Richard, who were dory mates, had baited and hauled their trawls twice that day. Then they had returned to the *Bridget* and gutted, washed, and dressed the fish. Captain Paddy had rendered their oil. Under the hot

August sun, sweat poured off Richard's face. Without a word, he pulled his clothes off.

"Come on, John," he said, nearly naked on the deck. "Let's go for a swim."

John stood and looked at his friend, almost dumbstruck.

"Are you cracked, b'y?" he asked.

"There's a shoal here, sure," Richard answered. Then he dashed over to the ship's rail and dove over the side. His body broke through the water silently and he glided through the ocean.

"I didn't even know he could swim," John said, peering over the railing.

"Go on, then," Captain Paddy urged. "Join him." He, too, looked down at Richard, who had surfaced now about twenty feet away and was splashing about in the cold Atlantic. The Captain smiled. Richard's sudden playfulness made him feel surprisingly good, too.

John glanced askance at his father, as if he, too, had gone mad, but then he stripped and joined Richard under the waves. In the water, they wrestled each other like children, and raced each other back to the *Bridget*.

*

At the end of the season, Richard and the rest of the crew spent a few days putting everything away, where it would stay until the next spring trip. This was on the merchant's time. They took down the heavy sails and folded them, then carried them up and stored them in Captain Paddy's premises. They upended the dories and brought them to the premises for storage as well. The trawls, of which there were hundreds of yards, had to be taken out of the tubs and put away. So did the tubs themselves. They took the pounds and liver butts apart. They took leftover provisions off her; there was a little sugar in the galley and some flour, but not much else, so exact in their planning were the Mannings. They gathered and washed the bedding before putting it away. They cleaned the entire ship, scouring every inch of her, believing that nothing shortens the life of a vessel more than dirt.

Finally, on the day he was to set sail back to Little Bay for the winter, Richard asked to speak to Captain Paddy.

"Sure, son, what is it?" said the Captain, sounding concerned at first.

"Well, sir, it's about Angela," Richard started, then stopped.

The Captain lifted his brushy grey eyebrows.

"Well, sir, well, we want to get married." Richard heaved a great sigh.

He must have been awfully nervous about this, thought Captain Paddy.

"Both of you, you and Angela have talked about this?" the Captain asked.

"Yes, sir, we have," said Richard, suddenly sounding braver. "We want to get married Christmastime."

"Well, son, you have my blessing," the Captain answered. He was thinking what a good match these two would be.

Richard smiled broadly.

"Thank you, sir," he said. "Thank you very much, from both of us."

CHAPTER EIGHTEEN

The year after their winter wedding in Oderin – all the weddings were held after the fishing season – Richard and Angela built a house on the hill in Little Bay, just up from Steve and Elizabeth's. Their custom, as old as anyone could remember, was that the woman moved to her husband's village upon her marriage.

Richard's sister Rachel had just finished her years working in St. John's; she had worked in a restaurant where Military Road curves into Gower Street, in front of the old Newfoundland Hotel. She wore a black uniform, not unlike those worn by maids in turn-of-the-century France, and she was very proud of it. She was good at her job and she worked hard. Although she loved her time in St. John's, she loved Little Bay even more, and there was never any question of her not returning home to marry and raise a family. Like her brother, she married a native of Oderin, Banks fisherman Jeremiah Abbott.

Everyone expected her to pack up her few things and move to Oderin. But Rachel would not hear of such a thing.

*

"I'm staying here," she said calmly when the subject came up in her parents' Little Bay kitchen one day.

Elizabeth, and Rachel's sisters, Mary Jane and Annie, all stared at her as if she had grown a second head.

"You can't stay here. You're getting married," Mary Jane said in a tone that suggested she was talking to an imbecile.

"I know I'm getting married," Rachel replied, still calm. "But I'm staying here."

Elizabeth furrowed her brows. "Not in this house, surely?"

"No, Mother, not in this house, just in Little Bay," Rachel answered calmly.

"Rachel, you can't stay in Little Bay either," Elizabeth said patiently. "You have to go with your husband."

"Mother, I love Jerry," Rachel said even more patiently. "But I've decided that we should live in Little Bay, not Oderin."

"You can't decide that," Mary Jane said petulantly. Goodness, Rachel was ridiculous.

"That's not the way it goes," young Annie said very seriously. Rachel ignored them.

Elizabeth drew in a breath. "Rachel, you know what you're supposed to do. Now, what is this all about?"

"Mother, why should I move to Oderin?" Finally a tiny crack appeared in Rachel's voice. "Jerry will be away all the time anyway. I'll be among women I don't know. I know everyone here. I should stay here. It only makes sense."

Elizabeth didn't know what to say to such logic, logic she had never heard before. "But I moved here when I got married," she said, sounding and feeling quite unsure of herself.

Rachel didn't mean to be cruel by what she said next. "And how often have you seen your own people since? Have you been accepted by the people here?"

Elizabeth had no answer. She felt a little hurt, but she didn't know where to direct it.

"Jerry will be awfully mad at you," Mary Jane said.

"No, he won't," Rachel said confidently.

"He might not marry you," Mary Jane persisted.

Rachel rolled her eyes skyward. "He's got more sense than all the men in Little Bay combined." Then she looked at her sisters and added sharply, "Don't you two have chores to do?"

The girls scooted.

"I don't know what your father will say," Elizabeth said finally, shaking her head.

"He'll get over it," Rachel said and picked up a dishcloth.

Elizabeth's eyes rested on her daughter. She felt her lips curl in a smile.

*

"Mary Jane was just here, and she says Rachel won't shift over to Oderin," Angela told Richard as the evening light closed in on them.

Richard smiled and shook his head.

"No, I bet she won't," he said at last.

"Well, what'll Jerry say?" Angela asked, looking worried.

"Not much he can say," Richard replied. "It's Rachel we're talking about."

Angela looked out the window from her chair and saw Rachel walk down the path. She was tall – like a Beothuk, some said – her long, black braid flopping on her back. Her head was held high, her walk quick and purposeful. She was out walking by herself at night. Not every woman would do that now, would they? Angela thought.

She thought of Steve and his caves filled with rum. And Richard always trying to get his hands on books. Whenever a schooner came from St. John's, he'd rush over and find out if they had any books on board, right desperately. What kind of a crowd had she married into? Then she chuckled. They were interesting, anyway.

And she liked living in Little Bay. She liked the spontaneous "times," often when the schooners and western boats returned from the Banks. People gathered in kitchens and danced. Richard played the harmonica and danced. What a dancer he was, light as a feather on his feet! She loved to watch him fly over the floor. He was like a spirit.

CHAPTER NINETEEN

The children came in quick succession. The girls were first, four in a row: Lucy, Monica, Bridget (named after Angela's mother) and Elizabeth, who they called Lizzie, named after Richard's mother. Then finally a boy arrived, Richard, named after his father.

But he was a sick little baby. He failed to thrive. They did everything they could for him. They kept him warm and fed him with a dropper because he couldn't nurse. They had Elizabeth work every kind of medicine on him she could think of. But he couldn't live. Although the house was full of children and every one meant Angela and Richard had to work that much harder, baby Richard was deeply mourned. His father felt his loss way down in his belly. It was like a gaping hole had opened up deep inside him and refused to close. Angela let herself grieve for three days, and then deliberately turned her attention back to her remaining brood. She had to, she decided. But Richard struggled. He felt caught between the baby boy he'd lost and the children who still remained with him.

At night in bed he cried for the little lad, as he called him. Angela held him tight.

"Come on, now," she said. "God wanted him. That's God's way. That's what God wanted."

She was able to accept it, but he found it hard. Surely God wasn't that greedy, he thought.

He healed a little when three more boys followed: Vince, named after Angela's brother, who fished out of Oderin and sailed the world over; then Jack, called after Richard's brother; and Patrick, named for Captain Paddy, Angela's father.

Next door, Rachel raised her children largely alone, as she had predicted, since Jerry spent most of his time at sea. He fished out of Gloucester in the States, and Nova Scotia, in addition to ports in Newfoundland. Rachel had eight children, including two sets of twins. One set, little boys, died as infants. The other set were Margaret and Jim, her oldest children.

The families on the hill settled into a routine, a seasonal round of activities that saw the men gone for much of the year and the women making fish in the spring, summer, and fall. Women rationed fruit and eggs through the fall so they'd have enough to make fruitcakes and figgy duff at Christmastime. In late winter they started to run out of vegetables; it got even harder to spare things along. Children went to school for a few years, maybe more if their parents could spare them from chores.

There were flus and colds. As the 1920s drew to a close, the dreaded tuberculosis that was sweeping the world visited their village, carrying Rachel's brother Jim and her daughter Margaret away. So many were sick and trying to cling to life. One winter, of the couple of hundred people in Little Bay, twenty-one died. The people felt helpless and cursed as they waited to see who the disease would take next or if it would leave them. Then finally as spring came, it disappeared.

Years passed. Richard and Rachel's mother Elizabeth died. Old Steve died. Their children grew.

Through it all there was always the threat of storms that would take their ships and men away from them. And for all its summer brightness and gentle breezes, there was always a sinister threat in the August air.

*

Strange things happened in August, especially on coastal shores and in the waters that surrounded islands like Newfoundland. August Gales are at least as old as the written record. The first recorded August Gale made herself known in Pensacola, Florida in 1559, when she drove five Spanish ships ashore. The first recorded shipwreck in North America occurred in August of 1583, when the *Delight* met her doom in a gale off Sable Island, Nova Scotia. Torrential rain and dense fog blinded the captain while heavy seas tossed the *Delight* to bits.

As the centuries passed, these summer windstorms kept on tormenting fishermen and vessels. In 1609, a "tempest" made its way up the Atlantic seabord, putting the vessels in a British convoy on their way to the colony of Virginia asunder. Two of the ships sank, while a third, the *Sea Venture*, was presumed lost at first. Eventually, though, she made landfall at Bermuda, where her crew was shipwrecked. After ten months on the island, they built two small boats and sailed to Virginia. Their story is believed to be the inspiration for Shakespeare's play, *The Tempest*.

Less than two decades later, the New England coast was struck by another August Gale, "the Great Colonial Hurricane." The Reverend Increase Mather wrote that there was "no storm more dismal." Indeed, the gale left many shipwrecks in her wake. In 1788, another wind blast destroyed a great swath of woods through New Jersey to Maine.

The Caribbean Islands to the south were even more vulnerable to the moodiness of August. In 1666, a howling gale smashed every boat along the coast of Guadeloupe, including a seventeen-ship fleet with 2,000 troops. The island's batteries, featuring six-feet-thick walls, were totalled and her cannons swept out to sea.

For five days in 1785, an August storm battered the Eastern Caribbean, from St. Croix in the Virgin Islands to Cuba. Over 140 people died from her impact. In 1813, more than 3,000 Martiniquais died when an August Gale swept onto their island. In 1831, almost 2,000 people in Barbados lost their lives to an August Gale.

The vagaries of August weather are known on the other side of the Atlantic, too. In 1456, Prince Machiavelli witnessed a tornado that tore across Italy. He wrote, "From confused clouds, furious winds, and momentary fires, sounds issued, of which no earthquake or thunder ever heard could afford the least idea; striking such awe into all, that it was thought the end of the world had arrived."

It must have seemed like the end of days in France, too, in August 1845, when a tornado all but destroyed the town of Moneuil. Between seventy and 200 people were killed by the tornado, which was between 330 to 1,000 feet wide, over a distance estimated between nine and nineteen miles. Another August tornado swept almost forty miles through the Jura Mountains in France and Switzerland in 1890 before running out of steam.

England experienced her highest ever rainfall in August, when more than nine inches of water fell on the town of Cannington in 1924. Seville, Spain reached her highest ever temperature on August 4, 1881: a shockingly uncomfortable 50° Celcius, or 122° Fahrenheit.

For the Banks fishermen of Newfoundland, late summer also brought the threat of August Gales. They said little, but every fishermen feared them. These gales were always in the backs of their minds as they walked to their schooners, sailed to the Banks, and went into their dories to haul trawls. When they were out there, whether it was drizzly, foggy, or even sunny, they kept their eyes on the sky and the horizon, ready for a sign, any sign at all of hurricane-fed winds.

Some of them had their worst fears realized on August 25, 1927.

CHAPTER TWENTY

Richard was still fishing with the Mannings out of Oderin when they bought the schooner *Tancook* in 1924. Captain Paddy had retired, and John Manning was now skippering their vessels. The *Tancook* was modelled after the famous Nova Scotia schooner, the *Bluenose*, and was built by the same people. Most schooners were made with "green wood," but the *Tancook* and the *Bluenose* were constructed with steamed timber. Although the *Tancook* would end up as a Banks fishing vessel, she was originally destined for a New York millionaire. Eventually she was sold to Jack Cheeseman in Fortune Bay, and then to the Mannings of Oderin.

The Mannings had done well in the years after World War I. The price of fish was good, and they'd enjoyed healthy catches. They sold their fish to and did business with Bairds of St. John's.

The *Tancook* was forty tons and carried five dories. It was Richard's favourite ship on which to sail, perhaps because of her beauty, perhaps because of the closeness he felt to his in-laws, the Mannings, who made up much of its crew.

As Richard baited his hooks with squid on August 20, 1927, he looked up from his work, noted the balminess of the day, then carried on.

*

In tropical Africa, a sea storm was developing. On August 21, fierce winds swept across the Atlantic, over to the Caribbean. Then they passed northeast of Puerto Rico, turning to the northwest, howling all the way. Over the next couple of days the gale snaked and screamed its way along the eastern seaboard of the United States.

Lacking ship-to-shore communication of any kind, the crew of the *Tancook* knew nothing of this. There seemed to be nothing untoward in the atmosphere, as is the case with most hurricanes. They kept baiting hooks, setting trawls, hauling them, unhooking fish, pitching them on deck, then counting, washing, gutting, and dressing them. They did all this like clockwork. Then when the *Tancook* was loaded down, they'd start the long trip back to Oderin. August was almost over. Captain John Manning was glad of it; he had his father's morbid fear of August and her gales.

Before dawn on August 24, the winds swept just east of Cape Hatteras in the United States. Then the storm passed by Cape Cod in Massachusetts. By now it was trapped in prevailing westerlies, typical of gales and hurricanes. It kept heading north, through New England and past the coast of Maine. Thus far it had caused minimal damage. Then it went through mainland Nova Scotia. It destroyed orchards, fruit, vegetable, and hay crops in the Annapolis Valley to the tune of one million dollars in losses.

More than 250,000 barrels of apples were written off. The gale brought torrential rain around mid-morning on the twenty-fourth which lasted until mid-afternoon. One estimate was that more than four inches fell in this time. Roads were washed out and railway journeys made impossible. From the first night of the storm until one o'clock the next afternoon, only one wire between Halifax and Yarmouth of the Western Union Telegraph Company was working. The lines at Maritime Telephone Company were down even longer.

By then the gale had crossed to Cape Breton. Barometers on the island showed that atmospheric pressure was falling rapidly. In addition, easterly winds had developed as the storm began to reach its full force.

It flattened buildings in Cape Breton and tore down telephone and telegraph lines. This meant that islanders could not communicate with the outside world, including Newfoundland, where the storm was headed. Ditches and pathways in Sidney, Glace Bay, and other Cape Breton towns were flooded. So were highways and railways, making transportation almost impossible.

Even worse, this August Gale had already shown its murderousness. She had sunk the *Joyce M. Smith* off Nova Scotia. The *Joyce M. Smith* was a two-masted schooner built in Salmon River, Nova Scotia in 1920. Her tonnage was 122.57, and she was 122 feet long and twenty-five feet wide, a big vessel. Her captain was Edward Maxner of Lunenberg, Nova Scotia, and his son William travelled with him.

Almost the entire crew of the *Joyce M. Smith* were Newfoundlanders. Fred and Andrew Barnes came from Fortune Bay. Charles and George Burbridge came from Epworth on the

Burin Peninsula. Robert Cheeseman and his stepson Philip Cheeseman were Burin Peninsula men, too, from Burin Bay Arm. Samuel Crocker was from Creston South, near Marystown. Arthur Dominick was a native of Belloram; so was Thomas Poole. It is unknown what communities James and Thomas Samuel Farewell came from. James and Murdock Hancock came from Pool Cove in Fortune Bay. Benjamin Hannaram (probably Hanrahan) came from an unknown community, undoubtedly on the Burin Peninsula. Cousins James and Thomas Hodder were from Rock Harbour. Archibald Keating and James and Samuel Warren were from Salt Pond, Burin. John Whalen, married with six children, came from Fox Cove. John Pike, a father of seven, was a Newfoundlander from an unknown South Coast community.

Richard knew a number of these men; he'd met them at the Hollett and Brinton premises in Burin, and he'd fished with a few of them. Angela knew John Whalen's wife, now widow, and she'd heard tell of many of the rest. Most of the men were in their twenties and thirties. The storm showed all of them no mercy as they fished and then struggled for their lives off Sable Island.

Not for nothing did the Nova Scotia newspapers call the August Gale of 1927 one of the worst in their history.

*

The storm turned its attention to Newfoundland, as if the island had been its target all along. It was in the wee hours of August 25 that the gale reached over to the island. With Cape Breton, Nova Scotia cut off, there was no warning. It started licking the Southwest Coast first, then swooping small boats out of the sea and pitching them on land or into the sky. They came crashing down in a hundred broken pieces, a man's livelihood lost. The storm aimed at wharves, and they crumbled as if on cue, falling into the water, where the next day fishermen could only stand onshore and stare helplessly at the sticks covering the waves. Then larger vessels were pulled from their moorings and masts torn from schooners. People looked out their windows and saw these things happen. Then they drew back in fear. They thought worriedly of the Banks fishermen out there somewhere. They said silent prayers or crossed themselves.

By now, the storm's force was full and its breadth was immense. It blew houses off their foundations all over the island. It blew down a church at Ship Cove. It tore up fences, pulled out trees, and shattered windows. It wrecked fishing premises, sent drying fish flying from beaches, and shredded crops that had been tended all summer. Its effects were felt in St. John's in the east, Port aux Basques in the west, and Fortune in the south. It seemed impossible to overestimate its maliciousness.

CHAPTER TWENTY-ONE

While they watched the glass in their windows crack and the cabbages in their kitchen garden blow away, the women of the South Coast worried for their husbands on the Banks. Angela was one of them. Around her were her four girls and the little boys. She thought the roof would blow off the house, but somehow it had held. She would make Richard take the second storey down when he came back; it was just too scary with that wind on this hill, exposed to the mercy of strong gusts. Where was he? Was he on Mizzen Bank? Or the Virgin Rocks? Or the bottom of the sea? Or being tossed on the waves like some toy doll? God, it didn't bear thinking about. What would she do with all these children?

Rachel appeared at the door, with her youngest two in tow.

"It's not fit, is it?" she asked bitterly, but it wasn't really a question.

Angela shook her head and kept staring out the window, as if she might see Richard walking up the hill if she kept looking. Rachel got two cups out of the cupboard and fiddled with the kettle.

"Might as well have some tea," she said. She sounded almost angry, Angela vaguely registered.

"It's we who have the worst of it," Rachel continued. "The women. We got the worry. Worrying is worse than the thing itself. Worrying is worse than doing, than going through something. Being onshore is worse. I've always thought that."

"I suppose you're right," Angela answered quietly. Rachel was always coming up with something, she had to hand it to her. She never accepted anything the way it was. "But there's nothing we can do about it," Angela said.

"And that's what makes me mad," Rachel said. "At least the men know what's going on. Right now, Jerry and Richard know if they're safe or not. We don't. You got to be some strong to be a woman."

"Rachel, girl, it's no sense being mad," Angela said. "It won't help them out there or us in here."

"And it's no sense waiting for him at the window either," Rachel said. "Come here and have a cup of tea with me. We've got some work to do later to get those kitchen gardens in order."

Angela left her waiting post and joined her sister-in-law at the table. She took Rachel's hand and squeezed it so they could draw on each other's strength. Outside, the August Gale was about to pluck Banks fishermen from their families, who had felt so safe only the day before.

The seas were "mountains high" now. All over Placentia Bay and elsewhere in Newfoundland, schooners and other vessels tried to make it into port. Many of them came very close. In one community, women stood in their houses and breathed long sighs of relief to see the western boat carrying their husbands round the point. Then, as it turned in to face the village, it listed and crashed into the sea, breaking into three pieces. The men went sailing into the air, then into the cold sea, in waves for which they were no match. Their wives and children onshore wailed in limitless grief, able to do nothing but watch their husbands and fathers die.

The *Annie Healey* of Fox Harbour, captained by John Mullins, was on her second ever trip. Affectionately known as "Big Annie," she sank in high seas just outside Fox Harbour on her way back from Point Lance Rock, where the men had fished before the gale bore down on them. All seven crew members died, and none of the bodies were ever found.

Indeed, the storm turned the South Coast into a graveyard that day. From Burnt Island, the *Vienna* and her six men were lost. From Rushoon on the Burin Peninsula, the *Hilda Gertrude* and her seven crew members were lost. The gale took the lives of the six men of the *Ella May* from Rencontre West in Fortune Bay, and the four men of the *Annie Jane* from Isle aux Morts, farther west. From Red Harbour, the *John Loughlin* and her eight men were lost. Though the news would not trickle in for days, and in most cases events would have to be pieced together, the August Gale of 1927 left villages of widows and orphans, and the only bodies ever found were those lashed to the riggings. Through the storm, Angela and Rachel waited and prayed in Little Bay, wondering if they would be among the grief-stricken.

CHAPTER TWENTY-TWO

Angela's brother, Val Manning, and Richard were in Dory Number 1 of the *Tancook*, and they'd made a late-evening run to the fishing grounds. They wanted to load up as fast as possible. There was no sense in drawing the trip out. As usual, they had gone the farthest away from the vessel. As they began the long row back to the *Tancook*, Richard was thinking that maybe they were getting a bit too confident, or too greedy. He knew Angela would tell him to take things as they came, not to hurry or rush things. He reflected on this now as he repetitively pushed his oar into the water. Life would be easier, he knew, if he took a page or two from her book.

Then he noticed that the winds were picking up, slowly but steadily.

"See that, Val?" he said.

"The wind?" Val answered, for he had noticed it too.

"It was a dead-calm night until now," Richard said.

"Dick, b'y, I hope it's not an August Gale," Val replied worriedly.

Richard nodded and said nothing, but his body filled with dread. By now, every doryman on the Banks had an inkling that an August Gale was on its way.

Richard bent forward and threw his whole weight into the oar. Both of them wordlessly rowed hard towards the *Tancook* and the relative safety it offered. As they got closer and the wind slowly gathered force, adrenalin surged through their veins. Underneath them, the swell of the sea picked up. Richard felt a hint of the sea-sickness his father had cured so memorably years before, but he ignored it and it quickly died away. Finally the ship was in sight.

John Manning was standing on deck. "Get aboard," he barked. Richard and Val were the last dorymen to return to the *Tancook*. They were careless with the fish, tossing it on deck and doing little else with it. How different the night had turned out from what Richard had envisioned when they were hauling trawls on a calm sea just a short while ago. Now most of this catch would land back in the water, and that would be the least of their worries. Making safe port was all they cared about now.

The wind beating on their backs, Richard and Val hauled their dory aboard the *Tancook* and tied it down. The other men finished tying down everything else. Although the full force of the storm hadn't hit, they were preparing for it. They were about an hour southeast of Trepassey. But they would have to cross open water south of Cape Pine to get there. This was a wild body of water, and one that triggered much fear under the circumstances.

John turned the *Tancook* towards Trepassey and asked Val to fetch some rope in case he needed to lash himself to the wheel.

"If we get a good speed up, we'll be home before the gale hits," he said to his worried crew.

As the vessel turned, the sails made their thunderous noise. Up top, there were loud claps, fast whipping sounds, rapid cracks, and then more violent booms as the sails carried the *Tancook* across the water. With her powerful sails, it seemed for a moment that the *Tancook* might emerge the victor of the night. She was a strong vessel, and they hoped her nobility would not falter.

Richard and Val stayed with John at the wheel. They said little. Their thoughts were of home. John thought of his father, Captain Paddy, and all the stories he had told of August Gales. So did Val. Richard thought of Angela and their small brood. She was strong, tough even, and she was pragmatic, but what would life for her be like without him? Outport Newfoundland could be hard on a widow with young children. A woman needed a man just as a man needed a woman. That was the way things worked. *It was broken otherwise*, he thought. As the wind whistled around him and the sails flapped overhead, he ruminated on this. What would Angela do without him? Her early widowhood was, after all, a very real possibility, although he'd never allowed himself to really think of it before. And if the *Tancook* were to sink, she would lose her brothers and her husband.

He thought of his own brother Jack who'd be there to help her. Jack was doing all right in the shore fishery in Little Bay these days. But Richard himself didn't want to die, not with a woman who loved him and all those pretty girls to rear, and his little boy, Vince, who followed him around like an adoring puppy. He loved the way the children stood around him when he played the mouth organ, tapping their little feet. He had never been happier. He felt

111

needed; he *was* needed. He felt as if he belonged. Then a sudden gust, stronger than the others until now, knocked him out of his reverie.

"She's picking up," John said quietly of the wind. He took his timepiece out of his jacket pocket and looked at it. It was nearly midnight. Then he looked at the sky. He still thought they could make Trepassey safely; they were getting pretty close. But he said nothing. He didn't want to tempt fate.

Richard was still thinking of his family in Little Bay. He knew that the wind would wake Angela. It always did. The second storey of their house was an attic where the children played, and it creaked and groaned in the wind. It would be making an awful racket this night, he knew. Angela would jolt out of sleep with a start, then rise, light a candle, and go upstairs to make sure the roof hadn't fallen in. Then, he knew, she'd check on each of the children. She did that when she woke up with the house noises. When he came home, she'd probably ask him to take the second storey down. This time he'd do it.

Then she'd go back to bed and worry about where he was – at sea or safe in Oderin – and she'd worry until he came home or someone who saw him in Oderin returned to Little Bay and told her he was fine. Neither of them had any way of knowing how long that would take. It was the same for all the women of Little Bay, his sister Rachel included, and every other village along the coast. Sometimes he didn't know how the women were able to do it.

John and Richard saw the evening's catch and the dorymen's hard work slide off the deck and back into the stormy waves. Gone was their insurance against the hungry month of March. But they didn't care. Richard was not a rich man by any means, but the wind and water had realigned his priorities. Cape Pine was in sight now. So were other schooners trying to make port: the *Mary Anne*, the *Cape Race*, the *Jane Bailey*. They turned northward as they rounded the point of land into Trepassey Harbour. It was almost 1:00 A.M. now, and in Port aux Basques on the southwest tip of Newfoundland, small boats were being smashed to bits.

Then the *Tancook* lost her foremast in a wild gust of wind. The long pole cracked in half, plunging into the dark waves and throwing the vessel sharply to port until she bobbed up again, almost as if nothing had happened. Her sails were like scraps waiting to be sewn into some order, and the foresail was half-sunk as the mast dragged it into the water. The schooner was virtually helpless now.

John was lashed to the wheel and he gripped it, trying with all his might to steer the vessel. As the winds howled and the rain began to come down in torrents, Richard knew the *Tancook* would be driven ashore. He peered at the shoreline, discerning the shape of the rocks upon which she'd be dashed. He saw that they were very near land. At that moment, the gale tossed him out of the *Tancook* and suddenly his legs were underwater, his mouth filled with wet salt. He'd been thrown from the ship – they all had – and now they were being pitched by the waves. He pulled himself above the water and shook his head, trying to discern the features of the *Tancook*. He felt like a child looking frantically for its mother. He saw with relief that Val and the rest of the men were close by him in the water.

Next the gale heaved them onto land, and they sat, and then stood on the rocky beach, coughing and spitting. The *Tancook* lurched onto the rocks and Val scrambled aboard her to release his brother from the wheel. John, his Cape Ann long blown away, stood in the rain watching his boat flounder in shallow water. "We'll get help towing her out tomorrow," he said.

"She's not beyond repair," Richard added, yelling over the screams of the gale. "Her hull is all right."

Men from Trepassey arrived over the cusp of the beach, ready to welcome the stranded Banks fishermen into their homes. They were good boatbuilders here, too, John knew, and he'd need their skills soon to replace the foremast on the *Tancook*. Richard kept looking back at the schooner as he walked up the beach and into the village. It was hard to leave her in the water, looking so helpless like that. It didn't feel right. He had grown to love that beautiful boat.

The next day, he returned to the Trepassey beach and saw the wreckage of small boats still splashing about in the ferocious wind. Though the storm had not yet quieted itself, the dorymen of Placentia Bay and Trepassey were already at work on a new foremast for the *Tancook*. Richard saw that dozens of flakes here were flattened and that the wind had cracked the mainmast off a schooner moored in the harbour. He wondered about the damage along the South Coast, in Little Bay, and elsewhere on the Burin Peninsula. *I don't suppose our roof came in*, he thought.

He imagined Angela and the children fretting about him. Dark-haired Lizzie, just like her grandmother, was the youngest girl, and she would be worried the most, he knew. Rachel would not want to be alone with her fear for Jerry, and she would take her children up the hill to Angela's. At least they could be together, he thought. But he did not envy them for their waiting.

CHAPTER TWENTY-THREE

The people of Placentia Bay, especially the Burin Peninsula, reckoned that the August Gale of 1927 was the region's worst natural disaster. Although they could recall many gales and many tragedies of men lost at sea in squalls and hurricanes, the oldest of the old people could remember none worse than this one. That fall, they put all the stories together and spread them through the bay. In kitchens and in fishing rooms all over, they talked of little else. They remembered the men of the *Hilda Gertrude*, who had left the Burin Peninsula community of Rushoon in deep mourning. They spoke of how the wives of the *Ella May's* crew had seen tokens, visions of their loved ones that portended their deaths, earlier that summer. Fate was cruel, they said, and merciless. The *Annie Healey* almost made it into Fox Harbour, everyone said regretfully over and over. But she hadn't; she'd been bashed to pieces by waves gone mad, and all her crew lost. It was as if the people hoped they could change things if they repeated it often enough.

Richard realized how lucky he, Val, John, and the crew of the *Tancook* had been that terrible night. If he and Val, in Dory Number 1, had been any later returning to the schooner, they might have perished. Any delay might have made a fateful difference. Or, if the *Tancook* hadn't been such a well-built vessel, made of the finest wood, or if John had made a mistake or two in steering her back to the island, their voyage might have ended in disaster.

When he thought of this, Richard felt deep down the vulnerability that stalked him all his life as a doryman. He thought of Robert Cheeseman of Burin Bay Arm who'd fished more than forty years, some of them with Old Steve, and of young Arch Keating from Salt Pond, who was just starting out in the Banks fishery and in life. Both of them were lost on the *Joyce M. Smith* out of Lunenberg, Nova Scotia. *They weren't even in their own country when they died*, Richard thought. Somehow the idea of their deaths in a foreign sea left a bitterness on his tongue. Their bodies weren't found, either, and never would be. Nor were those of any of their fellow dorymen, most of them Newfoundlanders.

Richard felt damned lucky, even blessed. He had spent his whole life in his own country, which he loved, despite its wildness and moodiness. He had often felt the presence of God in his life. It wasn't a strict religiousness, exactly. It happened sometimes when he danced, when he played the harmonica, when he looked at one of his children, when he loved his wife late at night. He wasn't sure what to call it. He wished he had more book learning, so he could give things their proper name. That was his one regret.

He didn't really get such a thing – this blessed feeling, this closeness to God – from his parents. His father wasn't religious. Old Steve's mother, Susan Spencer from Marystown, had been Church of England and not deeply religious; she hadn't drilled religion into her children. Steve said his prayers – Richard remembered how the Catholic men gathered to say the Angelus on the *Laura Claire* on his first spring trip – but it was a rote thing with Steve, a duty, like everything else. Richard reckoned that he knew even less of Elizabeth's relationship to God, except that she was devoted to St. Anne, the Micmacs' patron saint, who seemed even more important to her than God himself. He felt, though, that his mother had known God in a way his father had not.

Richard wanted to thank God for sparing him during the Gale of 1927, but he wasn't quite sure how to do it. He wanted to be a better man. But he told Angela of his intention and the reason for it, and she told him he already was a good man. "You'd best carry on being yourself," she smiled at him, and patted him on the back.

Then he took to walking into Marystown every Sunday morning for Holy Mass. There was no church in Little Bay itself. There never had been. There was a church in Beau Bois, a mile or two away. It was beautiful, set in the dense fir woods that surrounded the circular harbour that opened into Placentia Bay. Sometimes Angela took the children there for Mass. On the way they passed the small valley in Little Bay, where long ago Richard had seen the fairies and come running home frightened. Lucy and Monica, the oldest girls, told the story while the younger children listened wide-eyed and their mother chuckled. "That's why you need to have bread crumbs in your pockets," she said. "So the fairies won't bother you." The little ones looked up at her and nodded solemnly. Every time they passed the valley, their bodies stiffened.

Richard made solitary trips to the Marystown church whenever he was onshore. The walk was a long one. He traced the same route he had taken with Steve twenty years before when they'd set out for the *Laura Claire*, except now it was fall and he crossed the fjord in a dory, which they called the ferry. Then he went up the hill, glanced out to Shoal Point where his sister Mary Jane was now married to one of the Dobers – she had married a local boy and remained in Little Bay – and down the other side. It was some miles to Marystown, all alone, all silent. He loved this time. He spent it with his God, feeling thankful for all that he had been given and for being spared that awful night. He said a lot of prayers, too, for the men who had been lost and for the women and children they had left behind. He prayed fervently that Angela would not be left in such a situation.

CHAPTER TWENTY-FOUR

For the people of the Burin Peninsula, the year 1929 brought an event that towered above the August Gale of two years previous. It was, in fact, one of Newfoundland's greatest tragedies.

This was the tidal wave, although the term is not an accurate one, for the phenomenon had nothing whatsoever to do with tides. Instead, what happened on November 18, 1929 was a subterranean earthquake, a *tsunami*, the Japanese word for harbour wave. Deep inside the earth, a giant quake occurred, causing a kind of landslide on the continental shelf. Enormous waves, mountains high, rushed out from the epicentre of the quake and headed to the South Coast of Newfoundland. Then they rushed back, taking every ounce of sea water with them, draining harbours, and then rushing back again.

119

It was almost suppertime in Little Bay, and five-year-old Vince, Richard and Angela's son, was strolling up the hill towards his home. His belly started to grumble with hunger as he passed his aunt Rachel's kitchen garden, all picked over now for the winter. Soon his father would be back for the winter, and home until well after Christmas. He couldn't wait.

He saw his cousin Stevie, Rachel's son, come running down the hill. Stevie had just been in Vince's house.

"Did you feel the earth move?" Stevie asked.

"Are you cracked?" Vince asked, thinking that Stevie was pulling his leg.

Stevie shook his head. "Just now," he continued. "And the waves are getting real choppy." He pointed out to Mortier Bay.

Vince looked out and noticed that, yes indeed, the waves had gotten terribly active all of a sudden. But it was late fall and these things happened. Then he felt the earth tremble. He looked at Stevie, who stared back at him.

"See?"

Vince nodded.

"Let's go down to the harbour," Vince suggested, forgetting his hunger. "Let's see what's going on."

In the harbour, men walked out of their fishing rooms and gathered to talk of the tremor. In their hands they held nets and needles: they were repairing their gear for the next year, something that would take all winter. They were mystified as to what was going on. The boys ran around them, sometimes playing tag, sometimes listening to the men's conjecture.

Finally, Stevie's father Jerry spoke to the boys. He was in the shore fishery that year, and Rachel was glad to have him home, especially now that she had another new baby. This one was named after his father. "You two should get on up the hill for your supper," he said. "Your mothers will be waiting. Stevie, tell your mother I'll be up later on."

As the boys made their way to their homes, the sky seemed to lower itself to the earth and turned a blackish blue-grey. It looked fierce and threatening, even more than most November skies.

"Think there'll be a storm?" Stevie asked.

"Yes, I sure do," Vince asked, trying to sound brave. He hoped his father was on Oderin and not at sea.

"There you are," Angela said when her son came in the door. "You just about missed your supper."

She set a bowl of fish soup on the table for him. On the side was a thick slice of homemade bread with butter, also homemade. The girls had already eaten, as had young Jack, and she had fed Pat, the baby. Angela sat down at the long table across from her son.

"There's something strange going on," she said. "Did you feel the earth shake?"

Vince nodded. "Once, anyway," he said.

"Well, it shook more than once," she said.

"At least three times," Lucy called out as she dried dishes.

"Might be the end of the world," said her sister Bride.

"Maybe God is angry," Lizzie said.

"Maybe you're all being foolish," their mother answered. "But I think some weather is coming on. I'm some glad your father took that top storey down."

"You were always afraid of that," Monnie said.

"More like frightened to death of it," Lucy added.

Angela laughed.

Vince finished his supper. "I'm going back down to Uncle Jerry's fishing room," he said, moving towards the door.

"He's always got to be where there's something going on," Bride teased him.

Angela walked to the window and looked out. The waves were wild now.

"Vince," she said. But he was gone.

*

Vince was helping his Uncle Jerry mend nets when Stevie rushed in, out of breath.

"Aunt Angela told Mom to tell you to get your dory in," he said, his chest heaving as he tried to catch his breath.

Jerry put his net down and went to his door. He looked outside at the water.

"Good God!" he said.

He rushed outside and down the beach to his little boat. He plunged into the water up to his knees without even bothering about getting wet and hauled the boat onto the beach. Then he quickly threw a tarpaulin over it and tied it down as fast as he could.

Stevie and Vince watched from the fishing-room door. They were amazed. What they saw was a humongous wave in Mortier Bay. Then it headed into Little Bay. As it came closer, they scurried into the fishing stage and peered out the window. It was massive. They had never seen a bigger wave.

The wave pulled back and emptied the harbour. The bottom of the entire fjord was exposed and stayed that way for several minutes. Never before had either of them seen anything like it. "Good

God!" he kept saying. Over and over it happened. All the while, Vince and Stevie said nothing. They were too awestruck to feel scared. They didn't know what was going on.

All of a sudden, Vince remembered that his father wasn't home yet. Oh, no! he wasn't at sea, was he?

Then the snow started. It was accompanied by a northeast wind that brought a biting cold. The snow grew thicker and thicker. With the wind, it was getting harder to see. Before long, the peninsula was plunged into a full-blown blizzard. Jerry took the boys up the hill to their homes, wondering silently, too, where Richard was.

CHAPTER TWENTY-FIVE

The quake was felt in the Maritime provinces of Canada and as far west as eastern Ontario. The people of Delaware in the United States, well to the south, reported feeling it as well. The great Newfoundland trade unionist Sir William Coaker was at the Newfoundland Hotel in St. John's, and he noted that men on the waterfront were loading fish when they saw a tidal wave of six or seven feet. The schooners at the pier were grounded in the empty harbour, he said, and the water did not return for ten minutes. A schooner coming down the harbour was forced around in a complete circle, he wrote. Meanwhile, the breakwater at Catalina, Bonavista Bay was swept away, and a couple of dozen cracks appeared in the concrete and stone powerhouse there.

It travelled at almost eighty miles per hour. Like the August Gale two years before, communications were cut off. As luck would have it, for some reason the only telegraph line linking the

Burin Peninsula to the rest of Newfoundland had gone out of service before the quake.

The first accounts of the horrendous damage wrought by the quake came from the coastal boat SS *Portia*. The *Portia* was the first radio-equipped ship to visit the peninsula, five days after the quake on November 23. She was followed by the SS *Meigle*, a relief ship carrying doctors and nurses, two coastal boats, the SS *Glencoe* and the SS *Argyle*, and the revenue cutter, the SS *Daisy*. The stories they gathered were both frightening and sad.

All the stages and stores along the waterfront in Lamaline were swept away. The road between Lamaline and Lord's Cove was washed out. James Lockyer, an old man who lived on nearby Allan's Island, was "crushed by the sea" and later died of injuries. In Point au Gaul, eight people died. Elizabeth Hillier and her four grandchildren drowned in their home when it was pulled out to sea. Elizabeth Walsh, a widow, and Mary Anne Walsh, were swept away in their houses. Thomas Hillier and Thomas Walsh also died. All the community's fishing property was destroyed, including all the stages and stores, cod traps, and provisions. Three houses were flattened, and seventy other buildings were wrecked. The livyers were in a state of shock as they looked at the sight around them the next day. This stretch of coast was flat, and the people had built their houses close to the sea. They had considered it safe to do so.

In Taylor's Bay, the waves had been between 80 and 100 feet high. The Bonnell family was stricken with the loss of Bridget Bonnell and her child, as well as the two children of Bertram Bonnell. A child of George Piercey later died of injuries. The *tsunami* had left fifteen families homeless, and all the fishing property in the village was gone. The coal was swept away, too, as it had been in Point au Gaul. In Taylor's Bay, only five houses were habitable, out of the seventeen that had been standing before the quake. Homeless women and children had to go to neighbouring communities in Fortune Bay for shelter for the oncoming winter.

The people of Lord's Cove were left without their provisions that November. So were their neighbours in Lawn, St. Lawrence, and Corbin. More than thirty buildings in St. Lawrence were lost. The quake and its wicked waves took a house in Lance au Leau and all the fishing gear in the village, and it had swept Great Burin clean. It ripped down all the waterfront premises in Step-a-side, known so well by Richard, as well as a house there.

In Kelly's Cove, one of the more exposed parts of Burin, it tore down three houses and carried away Frances Kelly and her fourteen-year-old daughter. Besides that, all the fishing premises were destroyed. Similarly, the fishing premises in Collins Cove, Ship Cove, Burin North, and Burin East were all wrecked.

Port au Bras was particularly hard hit by the *tsunami*. No less than eleven houses were levelled to the ground. Six of the houses had been built on a breakwater and were carried out to sea en masse, leaving dozens of people with nowhere to live. Fourteen western boats were smashed to bits, all the dories and skiffs destroyed. So were the fishing premises, gear, and winter provisions. Even worse was the loss of life. Among the dead were Jessie Fudge and her three daughters, Gertrude, Hannah, and Harriet, and Henry Dibbon and his sister, a schooner widow who had been visiting him, Louisa Brushett Allen.

At Cape La Hune, on the western entrance to Hermitage Bay, Stephen Spencer lost almost everything, his home, shop, stages, flakes, and stores. So did William Parsons. The whole village was "in ruins."

Rock Harbour, too, near Burin, another place quite exposed to the sea, was swept clean. James Hodder's house was swept away, taking with it $500 in cash. The destitution was general. Adding to the grief was the fact that many of the bodies were not recovered.

The next day the blizzard turned into rain, falling in torrents. The winds came from the southeast and weren't as cold. Men donned their oilskins and rowed out in dories and skiff to retrieve what they could. They picked up nets, tables, chairs, a few bodies.

The SS *Daisy* and the SS *Meigle* reported that the people of the Burin Peninsula were in deep shock. Some of them were desperate, others lethargic, some prone with grief. Ahead of them was a long winter with no food, no homes, no clothing, and most of the fish they'd caught and salted swept out to sea. They couldn't bear to think of the next fishing season. They had no gear: no nets, boats, tubs, hooks, and no way to get any. Their relatives were dead, and in most cases they had no bodies to bury. They didn't know what to do.

In the middle of these black days there was a speck of hope to which even the most distraught people clung. It came from Lord's Cove, and the name of the community was not lost on those who heard and told the tale. One of the giant waves had dragged a tiny house hundreds of yards into the harbour. Sarah Rennie and her three children were in the house when seawater flooded in and ripped the house off land. They ran upstairs, trying to stay dry, as none of them could swim. They panicked and screamed as they were swept out the bay. The glass of the windows shattered as the water covered their ankles, then their legs. Then the waves threw them about mercilessly, and all four drowned.

After the storm, some men from Lord's Cove rowed out to the little house, half-submerged in water, with its bright white curtains flapping in the breeze. They hoped to find the bodies of the Rennie family. Instead, they found a baby in its crib upstairs, entirely unharmed. The story made its way up and down the peninsula and indeed through Newfoundland, giving survivors and all those who felt some sympathy for them a reason to keep going.

CHAPTER TWENTY-SIX

Angela spent yet another night worrying about her husband. Again she thought of her children; were they orphans? Lucy and Monnie were almost old enough to go into service. She knew people in St. John's who could help them get good positions. She'd probably send them there. Like herself and their Aunt Rachel, they'd do that for a few years before they got married. They were very pretty girls, Lucy with her dark eyes and skin, and Monnie with her sky-blue eyes and high cheekbones. They were almost grown now. But Patrick, named for her father, was just a few months old. He wouldn't even know his father if he died now. And Vince and little Jack ... well, boys needed their father. Vince would want to go fishing with Richard in five or six years, in the shore fishery, at least. He was six now and adored his father, following him everywhere, always asking him questions. Richard got such a charge out of him.

Where was Richard? That question had almost driven her mad during their fifteen years of marriage. It was always in her head, whenever there was any sign of weather, and many times when there was not. It always left her frustrated. It emphasized her powerlessness. There was never any answer to it. Not until she looked out the window or up from the turnips and cabbages in her kitchen garden and saw him coming up the hill. It was late now, nearly the end of November, but he might still be at sea.

They were strange events last night, awful strange, not like any of them had ever seen before. Nobody could explain it. Thank God the storm hadn't caused much damage. Hopefully it was the same in the other communities in the bay, although Little Bay was more sheltered that most. *It might be different around Burin*, she thought, where many of the buildings and houses were perched on bald rocks poking out into the sea, and farther up the bay, around Lawn where she had relations. No shelter there. They built their houses in that place to be near to the fishing grounds, but maybe it wasn't so safe there.

*

Angela would have been pleased to know that Richard was in fact onshore at Oderin. The *Tancook* had finished her last trip of the year and had done well. John, Val, and the rest of the crew were in a good mood, having returned to the harbour with a full load of fish. They eagerly looked forward to Christmas.

They were so well pleased with themselves that they didn't mind doing the usual end-of-season work, as back-breaking as it was, and even though they were exhausted after baiting their hooks and hauling their trawls almost around the clock for weeks on end. Around suppertime they were on deck with the *Tancook* moored, folding and lifting the mainsail, an onerous task, when they felt the first tremor.

"What the hell was that?" Val asked.

"It's like the earth shook," Richard said.

"Like an earthquake you get down south," John answered.

Like his brother, Val had been to the West Indies and had seen the destruction wrought by the high winds of fall hurricanes and sudden earthquakes.

"Be glad we don't live down south," he said. "They can do some harm. They can wreck a place. It can take years for a place to get back on its feet after a quake."

A couple of hours later, Val and Richard stood in the doorway of one of the stores of the Manning premises, having just put away the mainsail with the other dorymen. They had paused for a quick rest. Then they noticed the peculiar action of the waves.

Suddenly, Oderin Harbour was empty, clean and dry. They were looking at its bottom. Then, about five minutes later, it was full with a high wave. The men were amazed.

"I don't know what the hell that is," Val said.

Richard was bewildered, too. He was thankful that the waves weren't higher and that they didn't seem to be destructive. Like Little Bay, Oderin would be spared that night. He hoped they weren't worse anywhere else.

*

The subterranean earthquake off the Grand Banks that November night measured 7.2 on the Richter scale. The quake caused the sea floor to move several yards, causing the water to go back and forth for several hours. Some of the waves raced across the ocean at more than 800 kilometres an hour, as fast as an airplane. This speed took them far, far away from where they originated.

When a *tsunami* reaches shallow water near a coastline, its waves increase in height and become a mountain of water. It is at this point that harbours become empty and everything on their bottom exposed. But then the waves rush in at frightening speed, wreaking the kind of damage experienced by the people of the Burin Peninsula on November 18, 1929.

Tsunamis create massive waves, often fifty feet high but sometimes 135 feet high. Each wave is higher than the one before. The time period between waves is between ten and thirty minutes. Because of their size, they can be murderous. In 1896, more than 20,000 people were killed by a *tsunami* in Sanriku, Japan.

Japan is vulnerable to *tsunamis*, sitting as it does in the Ring of Fire, the prime *tsunami*-prone region that encircles the Pacific Ocean. Hawaii, a string of islands in the middle of the Pacific, the world's largest ocean, is very susceptible to *tsunamis*, generally experiencing one a year. Alaska, much farther north but also on the Pacific, has one about every two years. The *tsunami* that hit the Burin Peninsula in November 1929 was way outside the Ring of Fire, and the people who lived there had no way of knowing it was coming. They didn't know what hit them. Some of them thought the end of the world had come.

CHAPTER TWENTY-SEVEN

As details of the disaster trickled into Oderin, Richard and the Mannings readied the *Tancook* for an unexpected winter voyage. It was bitterly cold, with intermittent snow squalls and a stubborn wind coming from the southeast. A sense of help-lessness pervaded the air as they heard sad tales of dead women and children trapped in houses swept out to sea. Despite the weather, the Banks fishermen felt the need to render whatever assistance they could to the stricken people of the peninsula, so they hauled the heavy sails out of storage. They worked almost around the clock to hoist them and get the standard rigging in place. They took two of the dories out of storage and put them back on the schooner in case they were needed. They nearly froze as they did these things, but they wanted to do what they could.

Richard had sent word to Little Bay via another Oderin western boat that he was fine, that he had been on the island when the "tidal wave," as they called it, struck. He felt bad that Angela had fretted over him. She had worried for almost two days, until she'd heard he was fine. It was the same for his sisters Rachel and Mary Jane, and their husbands, too, and would be for young Annie when she married. He knew that Little Bay had been largely spared. But he also knew that friends in Burin and Lawn and Lamaline were destitute and homeless.

They sailed out of Oderin Harbour into a squall, worrying not about themselves but the survivors of the disaster. They said little, but each man thought of the horrors of little children drowning in their own homes. As they drew near to the Burin Peninsula they saw eerie signs of the *tsunami*. Wreckage floated by them: a window frame from someone's house, part of the lace curtain still attached, pickets from a fence, the stouts that had once held a stage in place. They didn't know if they should pick these things up or not. There was no protocol for such events in this country.

Farther along they saw smashed-up dories and part of the sloped roof of a house, a chest of drawers still intact, chair legs. It was the pieces of houses that caught in their throats, that quickened in their stomachs. The sights were horrific, but they could not help but watch. Most of all they feared seeing bodies, but the search for bodies was partly why they were out here. So few of them had been recovered, a fact that had added to the incalculable grief the survivors felt.

"Burin would have got some of the worst of it," Richard said to John, who was at the wheel.

"Yes. Rock Harbour maybe, where it's built exposed like that," John answered. "And Port au Bras."

"Some of those houses in Port au Bras are awfully close to the breakwater," Richard said. "Might not have been a good thing the other night."

John nodded, recalling that many in the community had died during the quake.

"All right, let's head to Port au Bras, then," he said.

Then Richard spotted a large white object floating in the water to the south. John pointed the *Tancook* right at it.

It was a house, a two-storey with all its windows broken out. It was battered, to be sure. But it looked sturdy, and it was still floating quite well all this time after the quake. They moved closer to it, tentatively since they didn't know how movable it was in the water. Although they didn't realize it, they were afraid, too, afraid that they might find the body of a child or its mother.

"The roof looks like it's in good shape," Val said. He had joined his brother and brother-in-law at the wheel.

"Come on, we'll row out to it," Richard said, getting excited.

Before long, he and Val had lowered one of the dories into the water, ignoring the choppiness of the waves in their eagerness to help. Then they rowed ferociously and came right up to the house.

"Be careful, lads!" John called out. But they couldn't hear him with the wind.

Richard and Val could see that the house still had some furniture inside. In the top storey there were beds and chest of drawers that slid here and there with the swell of the sea. They decided they should tow it back to Burin, where the local people would know what to do with it.

They rowed back to the *Tancook* to fetch ropes, which the other men threw down into the dories. With the rest of the crew,

Richard and Val spent the next two hours tying the house to the ship. It was a tedious and dangerous task, lest the house topple over on top of the dorymen. But it did not, and they sailed for Burin. As they slowly began the tow, Richard stood at the *Tancook's* stern, deep in thought. Then he went up to John at the wheel.

"John, b'y," he said. "That house belongs to Port au Bras. It's one of those houses that was by the breakwater, and I believe a fellow by the name of Fudge owns it."

"You sure?" John answered, glancing at him. God, it's cold, John was thinking. What a time for a disaster like this one.

"Yes, I'm sure," Richard answered. "I thought a lot about it when we were rigging her up."

"All right, that's good enough for me, Dick," the Captain answered. "Your memory never failed you yet as far as I know."

He changed course and pointed the schooner towards Port au Bras.

CHAPTER TWENTY-EIGHT

Port au Bras was one of the communities hardest hit by the underwater quake. Eleven houses had been swept away. So had fish, provisions, stages, flakes, outbuildings, and small boats. The worst of it, though, was the loss of seven lives, including three little girls, all sisters, with only four bodies recovered.

Whenever a schooner or western boat came into port, local people came rushing out to meet it. Children appeared on the shoreline, running about in excitement. Their mothers gathered and chatted, waiting for the ship to dock and expel its dories and dorymen. This time, as the *Tancook* pulled into Port au Bras, there was only a sorrowful silence. No one came to meet them. No one stared in wonder at the odd sight of a schooner towing a house.

When they were moored, the men gathered around Captain Dalton of the relief ship SS *Daisy*, who told them of the losses in great detail. The *Daisy* had towed one house to Burin and salvaged four schooners, which she brought back to Port au Bras. The Captain planned to fetch others, which he knew were on the bottom of the bay, when the weather improved, though it was late November now. He complimented the *Tancook* for the retrieval of the Port au Bras house.

"You'll find the people here are in deep shock," he said to sombre nods all round. "It's the same all along the coast. Some of them just sit and stare. They can't even speak. They can't believe what happened. It was so fast, so unexpected."

"What do the doctors and nurses say about their prospects?" Jack asked.

"Well, it'll take time," the Captain answered, not really sure what to say. "Shock is a hard thing." Then he returned to a topic with which he was more familiar. "There's lots of rebuilding to be done."

"It had to be winter," Richard muttered.

"Those people are really suffering without their own homes," Captain Dalton added. "They'll be without them till late spring at the very earliest."

"Well, we'll be off to find the owner of this house," John said, suddenly anxious to do something, anything.

"It's one of the Fudges, I'm sure of it," Richard said.

They doffed their caps at Captain Dalton, who boarded the *Daisy*. He was set to return to Lamaline and St. Lawrence, where the weather had prevented his earlier attempts to land.

The men of the *Tancook* bent into the wind and headed into the village. They knocked on the door of the first house they saw, and entered.

"We're sorry for your trouble," John began quietly. Dozens of eyes looked blankly at him. "Ah, we found a house, ah, at sea," he continued. "And we towed it back here."

"It was one of the ones on the breakwater, belongs to a Fudge," Richard said, sounding more confident than his brother-in-law.

"That's mine or my brother's," a hollow-eyed man said quietly. "If it's his, he won't want it. His wife and three little girls are all dead. They died in that house."

The men of the *Tancook* felt shivers travel down their spines. They hadn't considered such a scenario. The man who spoke showed no more interest in their find.

The room was filled with silence.

Richard looked around the little kitchen. There were people everywhere, some standing, some sitting, others leaning against walls. A jumble of people were crammed on the daybed. There were tired old men and women, sombre people in their middle years, and quiet children and youths. No one said anything. Most of them looked at the floor. There was a hint of shame in their way. But there was a strain of anger, too, threatening and bubbling just beneath the surface.

There was a cloud of sickness about the place. People coughed and sneezed. Then it dawned on Richard that most of them were homeless, their homes having been carried off to sea by the waves and now they were crowded in here, one of the few buildings left standing in Port au Bras. His heart sank way into his belly.

They looked cold. Some of them shuddered and shivered. Then he realized it was almost as cold in here as it was outside. They had no wood; they had lost that, too. Of course, he thought. They had lost everything. And the main window in the kitchen had been blown out. They had patched it over with sailcloth, but a fierce draft blew in. Some of the children had bluish lips. Mucus dripped from their little nostrils, but even the older ones made no effort to wipe it clean.

Richard suddenly remembered the bedclothes, sweaters, sweater coat, mittens, and caps the Manning and Jarvis women of Oderin had piled onto the bunks of the *Tancook* for the stricken people. "We've got some warm clothes aboard the boat," he said. "I'll go and carry them up."

He hoped to see their faces brighten at this news, but they didn't. Captain Dalton had said that the doctors on the relief vessels had left drugs for the people, but there seemed to be no cure for what ailed them.

In the forecastle of the *Tancook*, Richard grabbed a big canvas bag and stuffed it with whatever he could find: tea, bottles of molasses, twine, small nails. Then he ripped his holy medal off his neck – the one his mother had given him long ago – and threw it into the bag. It never occurred to him that the people of Port au Bras were not Catholic.

PART 3

CHAPTER TWENTY-NINE

He often laughed to himself at the irony of it. But other times it made him rueful. He had never wanted to go to sea. But what else were you going to do? But now he was getting offers from skippers all over the place. He was known as a hard worker, very responsible, diligent, and a top-quality salter. Salting was a real art, everyone knew, and not everyone could do it right.

Captain Hollett in Burin wanted Richard to come fishing with him. A skipper in Spaniard's Bay, all the way over in Conception Bay, made him an offer. Captains in Fortune Bay, Petite Forte, and St. Lawrence wanted him to join their crews. Once, he took the Warehams of Harbour Buffett up on their offer.

Being in demand didn't make him rich, though. Far from it. It made him less poor, he often joked with Angela. That was as much as a Banks fisherman could hope for in this country in this day and age. It was the Depression, too, and Newfoundland was as hard hit as anywhere else. The price of fish was low, and fishermen had to work harder to make the same money they'd made before the Crash of 1929.

He'd always wanted to live in the city. He associated the city, its busyness and great variety, with learning, something he also hankered after. But he could never see a way to it. How could a Banks fishermen, a doryman, set himself and his wife and seven children up in St. John's, after all? The older girls, Lucy and Monnie, would be in service in St. John's in a couple of years. Maybe they'd marry city men and their children would be city people, educated people with books all around them. But somehow he doubted it. Fate had played too big a role in his life.

He was forty-six now and the rest of the children were half-reared. Only Patrick was too young for school; he was only five.

Well, if he couldn't ever realize his dream of living in the city, he could perhaps achieve his ambition of having a shore job. His encounter with Peter Moulton in Burin after his first spring trip had put this idea into his head long ago. But that had been a bitter experience, he recalled. It wasn't possible then, not in that time, not with Old Steve breathing down his neck until the day the Lord finally carried him off.

But it might be now. He was his own man now. Even better, he had a wife who trusted him and supported his decisions. Whenever he'd changed schooners, even when he'd stopped fishing on the *Tancook* with her brothers to go with the Warehams, she'd thought it was the right thing to do. Angela was never afraid of change. She took life as it came, and her easy way had allowed him to relax somewhat over the years. Even during the hungry month of March in the Depression years, when they had to scrape the bottom of the flour barrel, he no longer paced the floor and bit his fingernails until they hurt.

When she said, "What's done is done," he nodded. Somehow they always got through even the worst of times.

Life as a Banks fisherman, a doryman, was a hard one and it would not have been his first choice. But over the years, he had even grown to like "pieces of it"; he often served as cook and delighted in making fish and brewis and tasty chowders for the men, and he took pride in being such a good salter, something he rightfully regarded as a craft. Frequently he was first mate, and many captains relied on his skills in taking soundings and reading the signs of the weather. Richard took pleasure in all this.

But the monotony, the constant hauling, and the sheer impossibility of ever getting ahead all made him weary. And his chest still tightened with the dread of the sea swell he had first felt when the ferryman took him to St. Pierre Bank thirty years before. His head still swished with the threat of sickness, which he always kept at bay, somehow, since it had been battered out of him a lifetime ago. He detested the salt air, the drizzle, the fog, the ice columns, and rain pellets that tortured the men as they hauled trawl. He detested the water pups that formed on his wrists and the pains that crept up his back, pains he had to ignore if his family were to eat that winter. At times, his innards twisted with the fear of snow squalls and August gales.

Worse, he hated the feeling that real life lay elsewhere. The life beyond his reach was of land, grass, paths, houses, wives, children, his harmonica, the church. He felt like a visitor to this real life, someone who was destined to spend most of his time in a watery purgatory. He had only occasional, fleeting leaves to the world. In a way, he felt like someone who was only alive part-time, when he was on land. He didn't tell anyone these things, not even Angela. He didn't have to, for she understood him.

CHAPTER THIRTY

In 1933 and '34, Richard fished with Jim Joe Farrell, his neighbour in Little Bay. Jim Joe captained the *Ronald W*, a fortyton schooner that was old and that Richard never quite trusted. His brother Jack had joined him on the *Ronald W*, and they'd fished foggy Cape St. Mary's and the St. Pierre Bank, where the dark spirit of their father seemed to overhang everything. That year the fishing had been poor; catches were low, and to make matters worse, prices had dropped even further. All over the world, the pain of the Great Depression was continuing to make itself felt.

Much taller than Richard and darkly handsome, Jack was in his mid-thirties but had not yet married. One romance had faltered because of his intended's disapproving mother, who had regarded Jack as too handsome for his own good. Now, however, Jack was engaged again to a girl from Spanish Room. He was building a little house on the bottom of the hill on the south side of Little Bay, just below Rachel's and Richard's homes.

The brothers were stowing the *Ronald W's* gear for the winter, hauling the mainsail to Farrell's stores, when Richard confided in Jack.

"I've got a mind not to go to sea next year," he said somewhat tentatively.

"What are you going to do instead?" Jack answered, laughing. "Become a gentleman farmer? A squire or something?"

Richard frowned. "I've got an idea. It just might work."

Jack let go of the sail. His brother had adopted that real serious way he had. He nodded to let Richard know he was listening.

"Well," Richard began slowly. "Look at John Power's place over there." He pitched his head in the direction of Power's premises, where the flakes jutted out into the harbour. "And Paddy Hanrahan's, and Leonard Hanrahan's."

Jack considered what his brother was saying. The three men Richard had mentioned had gone into business for themselves. Schooner captains brought their catches to them, where they washed and dried them, then had their women employees make them. Afterwards, the captains returned to collect it. John, Paddy, and Leonard worked for themselves, no one else. They were able to stay onshore year-round. Both of these things appealed immensely to Richard, as he explained to his brother.

Another alternative was to manage a premises for one of the larger fish companies. In Little Bay, Philly Walsh did just this for A.H. Murray.

"Maybe I can start out that way," Richard said.

"You're the best salter in the bay," Jack said firmly. "There's no disagreement on that. You could learn the women and young men how to salt right." Then he paused. "So why should you work for anyone else? You should go right into business for yourself."

"That might be hard to do right off the bat, though," Richard said. "I might need some money. Where in hell does a man get his hands on some money around here?"

Jack bit his lip and said nothing. His brother had a point about that. He was torn. These were hard times, very hard times. But he knew Richard was sick of the water and hated fishing. There had to be a way for this thing to work.

*

"Here it is," Jack announced, as he burst into Richard and Angela's kitchen a few days later. "I've got the answer."

"The answer to what?" Angela said. "You figured out how to stop winter from coming?"

He flashed a grin at his petite sister-in-law and jumped out of his boots, rushing over to Richard at the table having a mid-morning mug-up.

"What is it, Jack b'y?" Richard asked expectantly, laying his cup down.

"Here. 'Men wanted at Corner Brook building site'," he read from a newspaper clipping. "They're still hiring over there, even though they got the mill built. They're putting up houses."

"Where did you get that?" Richard asked, taking the scrap of paper and turning it over. He seemed more interested in the news stories on the other side than in the ad itself. He began to read aloud, "The Italian government – "

"Never mind that, Dick," Jack said impatiently. "Here's a way we can get some money."

A look of realization crossed Richard's face, and he nodded, at first slowly, and then more excitedly.

"Yes, b'y, that's what we'll do," he said.

"You're just home, and now you're off again," Angela said.

"Can I go, Dad?" young Vince asked. He had wandered into the kitchen after hearing the commotion.

"No, son," Richard told the ten-year-old. "When you're a bit older, you and me will work together. We'll go working onshore somewhere."

Angela smiled. She knew how Richard's father had beaten the seasickness out of him. She knew he would slowly and gently introduce his own sons to the world of work.

"Well, I suppose I better get the two of you ready," she said, referring to Richard and Jack. "You'll have to get on one of the coastal boats. I suppose they got somewhere over there for the men to stay. And I hope they got decent food."

"Corner Brook is being all built up, Angela," Richard said. "There's a mill there now. It's a big town. There's bound to be everything there."

"There's men going to Corner Brook from all over the island," Jack said. "There's plenty of work there."

"Maybe it'll rival St. John's one day for industry and such," Richard said.

A thought crossed his mind. Maybe, if it was a nice place and there was work there, he could move his family there. He glanced at Angela. Would she leave the bay? Yes, he thought, she would. He looked back at the table.

She sat down beside him. She glanced at him. Maybe they'd go live there, she thought, if it'd get him off the water. He could see what it was like there. There must be lots of families moving there if their men were going to work in the mill.

Richard brought his thoughts back to the money he and Jack would earn at the Corner Brook construction sites.

Angela spent the next couple of days darning their socks and woollen gloves and packing their clothes. Then she made piles of saltbeef sandwiches that would sustain them on their long journey along the South Coast of the island.

As the coastal boat carried them across Fortune Bay, then past Hermitage, the mouth of Bay d'Espoir, Grey River, LaPoile, and Isle aux Morts, Richard dared to hope that maybe he had left the Banks fishery behind as well.

CHAPTER THIRTY-ONE

Through the winter and spring of 1934, Richard and Jack and hundreds of other men from around Newfoundland laboured in the cold to expand the new town of Corner Brook. The company owned the townsite, as it was called, and it was responsible for building all the houses and roads there. This gave Richard a bad feeling. It was another variation of the merchant controlling everything, he thought. *At least we have our own house back home*, he thought, and no one could take Angela's kitchen garden away from her. If they wanted to, the company could kick people out of their homes here, at least in theory.

The town was growing so fast that construction of the town-site hadn't been able to keep pace. The homes there couldn't accommodate everyone who came. Plus, many Newfoundlanders with Richard's mindset didn't want to live there; they preferred to build their own houses outside the townsite. As a result, little homes sprung up haphazardly on the hills that surrounded Corner Brook and made it so picturesque. There was raw sewage in the pathways, though, and disease spread quickly: flu, fevers, tuberculosis, even typhoid. Richard decided that he would not take his family here. Maybe one day in the future, when the problems that inevitably resulted in a new town were sorted out. But that would be a long way off. Jack told him he was cracked for even thinking of moving here.

"You got your money now," he told his brother on the way home. "That's what we came for, not to become refugees."

"Jack, she's not much now," Richard said. "But mark my words, one day Corner Brook will be really something, a beautiful place. I can see it in the making now."

They had missed the spring trip with Jim Joe and the *Ronald W* but they didn't mind, for they had money in their pockets, a rare thing in their lives, and in the middle of the Depression, too. It was another thing with Jim Joe, but he would live with their decision. He was glad to get Dick Hanrahan, master salter, for the rest of the year. He considered himself lucky. He knew other captains, some of them on bigger vessels, had gone after Dick and made him offers. He was glad they were both from Little Bay; he had a feeling that Dick was loyal to men from his own community.

He was glad to have Jack, too. Jack's height seemed to give him extra strength and speed, which served him well on the Banks. He was able to row, pitch fish, and lift heavy sails with ease. The other men enjoyed his companionship, his energy, and his humour. Jim Joe knew that every bit of brightness counted out there in the dampness and fog that was their ever-present companion.

But their first trip to the Cape – and, Richard hoped, the beginning of his last year fishing – had not gone as expected. Jack was uncharacteristically slow emerging from his bunk, and then moving about the deck. In Dory Number 1, which he shared with Richard, he was listless and quiet. He got worse each day, so much so that Richard ceased counting fish the way their father had taught him, and instead obsessed with his brother's health.

When the *Ronald W* sailed into Little Bay loaded down, Jim Joe and Richard bundled Jack into Dory Number 1 and rowed him to the bottom of the hill. Then they carried him up to Rachel's house, where they knew she could doctor him. He was so tired, and his skin had a yellowish cast when they brought him in.

"It's TB," Rachel said after only a quick look at him. "He's got TB. Probably got it in Corner Brook." She looked down at him on her daybed, remembering her daughter Margaret, lost to the disease not long before. She glanced at Jim, Margaret's twin, standing next to his uncle and Jim Joe. His face was sombre. What could she do for Jack when she could do nothing for her own child?

Down below the hill, the other dories were reaching the beaches of Little Bay, where the dorymen would dump fish and the women would spread it in the sun to dry. Richard and Jim Joe walked solemnly back to the dory and then rowed out to the schooner and began loading her with fish. All Richard could think of was Jack. He didn't give a damn about all this hard work and slimy fish. He was sick to death of it. He wanted Jack to be part of the enterprise he planned. Jack, a young man who was going to be married next winter, had already built his house and was making furniture whenever he got a chance. Tuberculosis. Every bloody thing that could just had to go wrong.

He felt like a cork bobbing about on the sea, being pushed this way and that by a swell that just wouldn't stop. All around him were other corks: Jack, Angela, Rachel, his children.

CHAPTER THIRTY-TWO

Within a month, Jack's body lay in the dark earth in the shadow of the little church in Beau Bois. Rachel had stood tall and silent at her brother's funeral Mass, refusing to cry. She had cried floods for her daughter Margaret, and she would do it no more; she had learned that no good came of it. By her side was twelve-year-old Jim, equally stoic, and his little brothers and sisters, then Angela and her brood. At their side, Richard was quiet, too, seemingly stunned that the man with whom he'd climbed scaffolds just a few months before now lay flat and shrunken in a pine box. Jack's fiancée, Selena, however, sobbed pitifully, as if her life was over. She clung to her mother like a little girl. Jack's younger sisters, Mary Jane and Annie, cried too. Richard glanced at them across the aisle, numbly thinking that they'd do less of that as the years pass and life shows them what's what.

Although Jack was dead, the men of Little Bay and the Burin Peninsula continued to board their schooners, climb into their bunks, rise before dawn, gobble their breakfasts, and row out to their spots on Mizzen Bank or off Cape St. Mary's. There, while Jack lay in sacred ground, they let out their baited trawls and hauled them in, filling their little boats to the gunwales with fish. Then they rowed back to their schooners and unloaded their catch, counting every last fish, then washing, cutting, and dressing them, tossing their livers into the butts so that their captains could render oil. Jack was dead, but they kept doing these things. It seemed ludicrous to Richard, whose heart was full of a grief that would not lift. They kept on doing these things as if nothing had changed, as if Jack were still alive, as if his jokes and laughter could still be heard through the dripping fog that hung over the Banks. It could not be real. But somehow it was.

Back in Little Bay, Rachel plunged her long thick hands into the earth that surrounded her house. She laid down dried capelin in the hopes that it would help coax bigger turnips and cabbages out of the ground. She sent her sons to the beaches to fetch the shiny little fish when it rolled in the dusks of late June. Then she spread it carefully across the garden, showing her daughters just how it was done.

She got her daughters to make the bread now, as she spent more time in her kitchen garden. This was the only place she felt a lifting of some of the grief that dogged her every step since Jack died. It seemed her family were being picked off: her brother Jimmy, her little twins, her parents, then her daughter Margaret, and now Jack. It made her feel helpless, a feeling she was in no way at home with. Here in the garden she felt something of

157

Elizabeth's presence. In the texture of the soil, she felt her mother's warm hands; in the graininess of plant roots, she recalled her strength. Longing for Jack the way she did, she summoned it now.

She checked on her trees. The plums would be juicy and fruity, she knew. Even the apricots would yield tasty flesh and medicine that might protect them from the awful diseases that kept carrying them off. Again she thought of her mother, wishing she were still here to see her daughter's garden grow, to see her children grow.

One morning, Rachel looked out her kitchen window to see Richard and Angela's boys running about in her garden. Young Jack and Patrick were chasing each other in the rows of cabbages and potatoes she'd been working so hard on. They were her family's winter provisions, she reminded herself, their insurance against the hungry months.

She balled her large hands into a fist and felt anger rising in her chest.

"What is it, Mom?" Rachel's eldest daughter had joined her at the window. "Oh!" she added as she saw her cousins weave in and out of the plants. They seemed to be taking as much care as little boys could, but not as much as was necessary in a vegetable patch.

Rachel heaved a sigh of disgust.

She tore her apron off and rushed toward the door.

"Get out of that!" she shouted at the children from her doorway. By now young Patrick had sliced through a cabbage with his boots. Rachel saw this and began to chase him.

"Get out of here!" she cried. "Go on home! And don't ever do that again!"

Jack and Patrick were afraid now, and they ran away as quickly as they could. Then Rachel stood in the middle of her garden, her hands on her hips, surveying the damage. After a minute her daughter joined her.

"It doesn't look too bad, Mom," the girl offered.

"I know, I know," Rachel answered. "That one cabbage is ruined. I think Patrick fell onto it. Maybe I can use it tonight. It wasn't just the cabbage. It's ..."

Rachel didn't continue, and her daughter took her hand. Then the two of them bent over and began straightening out the damage the boys had done.

As they were finishing up, Rachel saw Richard coming by on his way down the hill. She hadn't realized he was ashore. The *Ronald W* must be in.

"Dick!" she called out. When he came over, she blurted out, "Your two youngest tore up my kitchen garden this morning. They were in here running around, tearing up my cabbage. Can't they play somewhere else on this hill?"

Richard was quiet. Rachel had noticed how withdrawn he'd been lately, since Jack died. Then he said, "Rachel, they won't even be on the hill next year." And he walked away, leaving his sister and her daughter mystified. He was baffled himself. He had heard the words come out of his mouth, but he had no idea what they meant or where they had come from.

CHAPTER THIRTY-THREE

Richard had no intention of going to sea in 1935. This was the year he would start his shore enterprise. He figured if the other local men could make a go of it, so could he. Angela supported his idea and urged him to give it a try. She liked the idea of having him at home more often. She thought it would be good for the boys in particular. They were all at an age when they needed their father around them more now. The two of them knew it was the middle of a Depression, but they banished such thoughts from their minds and tried to cling to optimism.

Young Vince, eleven now, was still in the habit of going everywhere he could with his father. He was with Richard in front of the premises Philly Walsh ran for A.H. Murray when a man called his father over and asked him if he'd like to skipper the *Josephine Walsh*, a fifty-three-ton schooner, that year. The vessel was brand new, having been built just that year.

"No," Richard answered. "No, I'm staying ashore this year." He smiled. It was the first time he hadn't gone fishing since he was nine years old.

A few days later, when they were getting ready for the spring trip, the Farrells asked him if he would captain the *Ronald W*, the schooner he'd fished from with his brother Jack for the past few years. It seemed that he had better choices now than he'd ever had, if he wanted to go to sea. But he didn't, and he told the Farrells no.

When he told Angela this, she was surprised at his determination.

"Are you sure you're doing the right thing?" she asked. "Lots of fellows would want to be skipper. You'd get a better take."

"Yes," he said. "I know. I thought about it. I knew I'd get offers like that this year. I had one or two before. But my mind is made up. I want to go into business for myself."

"All right," Angela said. "Then do it."

Richard smiled at her.

"If it doesn't work out, I'll take the Farrells up another year, or somebody else with a better offer," he said. "But I want to give this a try."

"I know you do," Angela said. "Go on then, see what happens."

That night at the supper table, Richard looked around at the faces of his children as they ate their bread, potatoes, and fish. It had been another long, hard winter. Fish prices were low, very low, the worst in his memory, and the Depression dragged on. He'd had to catch more fish just to get half the money he'd made before hard times hit, and that was impossible to do in 1934 when catches on the South Coast were low.

Lucy and Monnie were in service in St. John's now, Angela having secured good placements for them. The remaining children were pale, with dark circles framing their eyes. On his right was Bride, who suffered badly from asthma. She was going to spend the spring and summer in Oderin helping her grandmother Manning and uncles. Young Lizzie, the face and eyes of his own mother, would likely join her there next summer when she was a little older. She was soft and sensitive, and he felt a special protectiveness towards her. On the other side of the table sat Vince, energetic, always ready for the next adventure, and young Jack, who would be a great student if Richard could somehow give him the chance to stay at his learning. Then little Patrick, not even six years old yet, and all skin and bones. *He'll probably be tall and skinny*, Richard thought. *The lad could sure use a little meat on him*. Richard recalled that the only hunger he ever experienced as a child was a result of seasickness, not lack of food.

Things had never been this precarious in Newfoundland before the Depression. The island had lost its independence and was being ruled from Britain again, and not for the better, from what Richard could see. Now he wondered what would become of their little country.

They said little as they ate; they all seemed to be concentrating on their food. The last few weeks had been particularly hard. They had run out of vegetables; all that was left now was some potatoes. Angela had been forced to send the children to school on lassie bread, which they'd also had for dinner and their mug-up at night. It was the same with every house in the harbour. People were still dying from tuberculosis, but they hardly talked about this now. As February turned into March, food seemed to become more and more important to them, to the point of obsession.

True to his word, Richard stayed ashore through the spring and much of the summer, trying to make a go of his premises. He attracted customers, some of the local skippers, but it was slow going. He was indeed the best salter in the bay, but word had to get out that he was in business. Besides, most captains already had arrangements made with other salters, or the wives of the dorymen would cure their catch. Another problem was that the weather was poor for drying fish; there were many damp days in 1935, and few that were optimal for making fish.

One day in early August, Richard was on the Marystown waterfront when Captain Paddy Walsh approached him. Captain Paddy was an old friend of Richard's family, respected by everyone in Little Bay, and a skilled skipper. In turn, he had the highest regard for Richard's talents at sea. Once or twice over the years, Richard had fished with him. The Captain again gave his sympathies for Jack's death the year before. Like Richard, the unexpectedness of it had stayed with him.

"Dick, I've been meaning to speak to you about something," the Captain said after a minute of respectful silence had passed. "I need some help with something, something important, and you're just the man I'd go to."

Richard nodded, growing slightly concerned.

"It's James, my oldest," Captain Paddy continued. "It's his first time out. He'll be skippering the *Mary Bernice*."

Richard nodded. He knew the ship well. She was a western boat, weighing no more than thirty tons, a small schooner with only two dories. She had been built only a few years before. Richard thought she was solidly built, ready for any seas, not like the aging *Ronald W* that he'd sailed in for the last time.

"She's a good little ship," Richard told the Captain. "He'll do well in her." He couldn't fathom what was bothering Paddy.

"He will, Dick, he will," the Captain agreed. "But he's young, only twenty-three. It's his first time out. It's August, and you know what that means."

He did. They all did. The memory of the 1927 gale was still raw in their minds and hearts.

"His mother worries about him," the Captain added.

And she's not alone in that, Richard thought.

"I'd really like for you to go with him," Captain Paddy finally said. "To act as his first mate, but to train him in, really."

Richard started to shake his head.

"We ... she wouldn't worry then, not with you there," Paddy added.

"Captain Paddy, I've got plans to stay ashore the rest of this summer," Richard said. "I've been making fish, and I'll be making more – "

"I know, Dick," Paddy interrupted. "But it's just one trip, his first, that's all. It's only a few weeks, less, I'd say."

Richard hesitated. He realized he'd get offers like this all the time and that he'd have to learn to stand firm.

"I'm very sorry, sir," he said finally. "But I got a customer now, and I'm bound to get more. I've got to stay here and mind my premises. I can't help you."

Captain Paddy looked downcast, even hurt, and this was not lost on Richard, whose shoulders began to slump a little.

"Would you even think about it?" the older man asked.

"All right, I'll think about it," Richard replied. "But there's more men around than me willing to go to the Banks. It's one of them you should be talking to. Don't let Mrs. Lillian get her heart set on it."

Captain Paddy tipped his hat at Richard and smiled as he walked away. Already his worries about his son's first trip as skipper were easing. His wife Lillian would feel the same way.

CHAPTER THIRTY-FOUR

The next morning, Richard was at his little premises before dawn. He looked around at the tables and knives and smelled the fish guts and blood and the oil that sat in the barrel. He watched the blackbacks dive at the water that pooled around the stouts holding up the flakes in the harbour. He looked down at the bottom of the bay, where the woods were green and thick, then to the little valley where he'd seen the fairies. He shivered at the fear-filled memory of it. He turned his back on it and peered into his fishing room piled high with salted fish, salt crumbs on the plank floor. A collector boat would be by sometime later that day. He wished he had more fish. But that was all he had. He knew Philly Walsh, in the employ of A.H. Murray, had a lot more. So did Paddy Hanrahan, a distant cousin, who was working for himself.

He furrowed his brow. Everything was spotless here. There was nothing to do, and there was enough of Old Steve in him to hate enforced idleness. His stomach growled, reminding him that he hadn't eaten yet. He looked at the position of the sun and noted that it was after eight now. He started for the hill and some breakfast. If anyone had met him they would have seen a grim look in his eyes.

When he was near the top, he saw his youngest son in his sister Rachel's kitchen garden. He remembered Rachel's harsh words from the summer before, when Patrick and young Jack had torn up her cabbage with their running around in there. Rachel was right. Those vegetables were food, food they depended on to survive. Why couldn't those children learn?

He hopped Rachel's fence and rushed toward his son. Then he pulled the child up by his collar, taking him completely by surprise.

"What the hell are you doing in this garden?" he yelled.

Patrick was stunned into silence, his great green eyes staring up at Richard.

"Answer me!" Richard shouted. Then he dropped the child to the ground and kicked his bony little hip. The boy curled himself into a ball and cried out. Then he began whimpering, afraid that more blows would come. But none did. When he realized he had nothing else to fear, he started to bawl.

As Richard turned toward his own house, Rachel's husband Jerry, home from fishing out of Gloucester, Massachusetts, burst out his door.

"I saw what you did to that child," he shouted angrily.

Richard's eyes narrowed. He said nothing.

"If I ever catch you laying a hand on one of your youngsters again, or any other youngster for that matter, I'll kill you, so help me God." Jerry's face was purple-red. He bent down and pulled young Patrick to his feet. Rachel stood in the doorway and stared hard at her brother. Richard's eyes met hers. The air between them was thick with the ghost of their father. Richard looked back at Jerry, who held little Patrick's hand.

"So help me God, I'll kill you, I mean it," Jerry repeated.

Richard spun on his heel and walked out of the garden, not looking back. He trudged up the hill alone, bent over as if he were carrying a cross.

When he reached his own house, Angela greeted him at the door. She said, "Ah, there you are, Dick. Have some tea and bread. It's right out of the oven. Lizzie helped me with it. She's getting to be some baker, I tell you."

"Thanks," her husband said sullenly, his voice low. He sat down abruptly and took a huge bite of the bread as soon as his wife handed it to him. He ate quickly, looking at the table.

"Well, b'y, there's nothing stopping you from eating when you're hungry," Angela said.

Richard threw a look at her.

His wife stood over him, smiling and wiping her hands on her apron. "I don't mind you taking up space in my kitchen, as long as you move when the girls sweep the floor," she said happily. She wasn't going to let his gloom interfere with her bright summer's day.

She chatted with Bride and Lizzie as the three of them washed the breakfast dishes, beat the rugs, lugged buckets of water, and gathered the bedclothes to be laundered. As they went about their chores, they created the energy of a tornado. *Is it like this every morning?* Richard wondered. He noted their efficiency, that they

168

did all these things without talking about them, and decided that, yes, it was.

Richard sat at the long table, shifting only when Bride needed to sweep the floor beneath his feet. Then there was a lull in all the activity and the girls seemed to disappear briefly.

"Angela," he called out. "Angela!"

"Yes?" she answered from the pantry out the back. Then her chestnut-brown head appeared around the corner. The twinkle in her eye coaxed a smile from him in spite of himself. He heard the sound of her laying a heavy container on a shelf, and then she joined him at the table. She took his hand and looked at him expectantly.

After a minute he spoke. "I'm going on the *Mary Bernice* for Captain Paddy next week," he said at last.

"What are you doing that for?" she asked. "We can get by."

Richard shook his head. "It's not just that ... I ..."

"You just feel like you got to do it," Angela said. Her words were more of a statement than a question.

He nodded. "Yeah, something like that."

"Well, I suppose it's only one trip," she said, ever practical. "He'll probably make you a good offer, Captain Paddy. Sweeten the pot a little." She smiled.

"Oh, he will," Richard said. "He as much said so. He's wanting me to do it as a favour." Then he stopped. "And I suppose it would be only one trip. I suppose. My last, I hope."

"We could use the earnings," Angela said brightly.

They sat at the table, Richard's sombreness refusing to lift.

"Angela," he said. "If anything ever happens to me, take the boys into St. John's so they'll get a good education."

Angela started at his words. Then she laid her hand on his arm, but he was still and she could not reach him. It was as if an impermeable curtain had descended between them.

CHAPTER THIRTY-FIVE

With young James Walsh skippering the *Mary Bernice*, Captain Paddy would be captaining the *Annie Anita* not too far away. He planned to take his two youngest boys, Jerome and Frankie, on the *Annie Anita* for the adventure. Unfortunately, one of them, Frankie, was prone to seasickness. Captain Paddy hoped the boy would grow out of it, for he wanted all his sons to follow him into the Banks fishery as captains someday.

The Captain's wife, Lillian, had been wistful, thinking of little Frankie go off to sea. This was an important time for her family. Things were changing so fast, with James becoming a captain himself now. That night when the *Annie Anita* was moored in Little Bay, Lillian asked James to fetch both of the little boys and bring them home to spend the night with her. They could join the schooner in the morning, she reasoned, and it'd be so nice to have them spend the last night before their trip at home. But when James peered into the *Annie Anita's* forecastle to find them, his little brothers were sound asleep. He thought about his mother's request, and then decided not to disturb them. He returned to his mother's home alone. She was disappointed, but accepting. "That's all you can do, son," she told him. "At least they're getting their sleep."

Lillian's relatively serene mood changed the next morning after breakfast. The day dawned bright and still, a beautiful late summer morning. It was a fine day to set off for the fishing grounds, everyone in the community said. The harbour was full of activity as men readied themselves for a trip to the Banks, one of the last of the summer. Thoughts of August gales were far from their minds under the hot sun as the month drew to a peaceful close. They had to keep optimism at hand in the business they were in.

But as Lillian sipped on her tea on the night of the twentieth with Captain Paddy, she heard an odd sound at her window, a small scattering noise on the pane of glass. There was no wind, none at all. The night was calm and clear. But, in spite of that, some sand and grass had flown up and hit the window. As an occurrence in nature, it was inexplicable. But the people of Placentia Bay knew the phenomenon as an omen. A bad omen. Lillian was suddenly filled with foreboding. She knew she was helpless to do anything about it. She stood at the window and looked at the ground, hoping against hope that she had imagined the sound, but she knew she had not. In the otherwise cloudless sky there was an inky black cloud, adding to Lillian's sense of foreboding.

She mentioned the omen to her husband, and he reassured her with a laugh that it was just a little whirlwind. Those things happened sometimes, he said. But she could not dismiss it so easily. Although Captain Paddy was ready to sail in the *Annie Anita* that night, Lillian asked him to wait. She feared something terrible was going to happen. He acquiesced. He didn't want her fretting, and one night wouldn't make that much of a difference.

The next day she saw her husband and son off to their respective boats, giving them kisses and hugs as she walked them down the path that led from their house. After they left the house – James to walk to Marystown to meet his vessel – Lillian sat down, looked at her youngest, a child of four, playing with a spinning top on the kitchen floor, and started to worry.

*

On the morning of August 20, Richard picked up his canvas bag, which lay waiting for him in the doorway of his home. It contained his oilskins, freshly dipped for this trip, a sweater coat Angela had recently mended, and a few odds and ends that he'd need on his voyage to the fishing grounds. They'd likely be fishing off Cape St. Mary's, Captain Paddy had told him, for the area was one of the Walshes' favoured spots.

On the top of the hill, Angela stood in a little meadow that fringed her kitchen garden. She watched Richard begin his journey to Marystown, where the *Mary Bernice* was moored and waiting for him. His canvas bag slung over his back, he walked slowly towards the harbour in his Kingfisher boots. *He's usually quicker on the feet than that*, Angela thought of her husband, who was, after all, one of the best dancers in the bay. Then she recalled that he'd been dragging his feet altogether lately, maybe even since Jack died, but perhaps even more lately. She watched him pass Rachel's house. This was her habit, to watch him almost until he disappeared from view, no matter how much work she had waiting for her back at the house. It was her way of passing on good luck to him, though she never told him that. She watched him although he never, ever looked back, not once in their nearly twenty years of marriage. He probably didn't even know she watched him. She didn't mind, though. Once he had a job of work on his mind, that was it. There was no room for anything else. He was like Old Steve that way. Now he was at the bottom of the hill. She took a few steps forward to keep him within her sight.

Then the strangest thing happened. He stopped, turned around, and stood there looking up at her. He didn't move; he was as still as a frightened deer. He was like that for a moment, his eyes on hers so far away. They stood that way, far apart, looking at each other. Then Richard turned back towards the harbour, where Rachel's son Jim was waiting for him in a dory to row him to Mooring Cove.

After she could see him no more, Angela stayed at the edge of her garden, focused on the spot where her husband had frozen, staring up at her. It was the strangest thing, she thought. Shivers went up and down her body, despite the late summer heat, and she felt the threat of a lump in her throat. But she didn't want to dwell on it. There was no point thinking about oddities. She spun on her heel and marched towards her house. She had a mountain of laundry to tackle.

From inside the house, her son Vince watched her. He did not tell his mother that he was thinking of something that had happened to him and his little brothers the previous fall. They had been in the bottom of Little Bay on their way back from Beau Bois when they saw their father in his leather boots, green wool jumper, and windbreaker. He stood at the edge of the woods in the middle of a path, quite still, not far from where some men were digging for clams. The boys rushed towards him but he disappeared. He had not been there at all, the clam-diggers told them. Sure enough, he was back in Little Bay. What the boys had seen was a token.

CHAPTER THIRTY-SIX

The *Mary Bernice* sailed for Cape St. Mary's at midnight, as was the custom in the Banks fishery. Richard stood on her deck with young Captain James Walsh under the roar of her sails in the cool night air. As they moved out into Mortier Bay, passed the mouth of Little Bay, and finally reached Placentia Bay, the unceasing thunder of the sails rang through the night. Richard found some reassurance in the great claps and licks overhead. The *Annie Anita* was not far up ahead, and they easily caught up to her. Then the two vessels headed for the Cape.

With dawn still a whisper, they anchored in a little cove north of the Cape and put their dories over the side. Then they jigged for squid. They needed bait; the crew had run out on the last trip. Richard was in a dory with Billy Reid, his close friend from Little Bay. In a dory alongside him were the rest of the *Mary Bernice's* crew, Dennis Long of Fox Cove, and Michael Farrell, another neighbour from Little Bay. Richard held a line in each hand, waiting somewhat impatiently for the tug that would signify a bite. On the end of each line were two hooks welded together back to back; the idea was that the shine would attract squid, though very often it hooked young cod, herring, or lance. No matter, though, they could use any of it for bait. Handlining was slow work that day, but they finally had sufficient bait to head back to their western boat.

Richard began counting the hours until he could go home. He was starting to feel that he was too old for this, a thought that had never quite come to him before. He had dropped a block of ice on his hand the previous year's fishing season and it ached now. He figured it was rheumatic and that handlining was probably not the best thing for it. Rachel had put a dozen poultices on it this many months, but it had never quite healed.

On the Cape, the southeasterlies usually associated with late fall and early winter had already arrived this year. There was just no predicting the weather at this place, Richard reminded himself. It was probably sweltering on the Placentia Bay islands or on the Southern Avalon Peninsula that led to the Cape, but this place had its own mind. The autumnal winds brought the thick fog and damp drizzle for which the Cape was known.

Richard knew there were many vessels around them, though the curtains of fog rendered them invisible half the time. Anything from dories to western boats to 200-ton schooners could be out there, and he cautioned Captain James to remember this. They still had no radios in the Banks fishery and could communicate with each other only through flags, lights, or by voice. Every few years, larger ships ran over dories or other small boats, and it was incumbent upon skippers to take every care to avoid it. Some did, but others did not.

They were quite near the Cape itself, probably the closest Richard had ever been. The loud ferocious squawks of the Northern gannets rang through the dense air. They were huge white birds with wingspans of nearly six feet, and black eyes that made them look like they were wearing bandits' masks. The boys would get a charge out of them, Richard said to himself, smiling as he thought of his sons. He would tell them stories of how foolish men had fallen to their deaths trying to climb onto the cliffs to get close to the birds. Others were convinced there was buried treasure in Golden Bay and near St. Bride's and in other places near the Cape. Adventurers came and went, trying in vain to find it. It reminded him of Angela's stories of the alleged treasure in Oderin. He smiled.

There were literally thousands of gannets here, perched on Bird Rock, where they came to breed each year. They shared the dismal spot with pretty, ivory-coloured tickle-aces who clung to rocks and guarded their little eggs as best they could. There were turrs here, too, with their great black bodies and tiny wings, giving them an almost prehistoric look, and sometimes little puffins, the clowns of the North Atlantic.

The birds were like them, the Banks fishermen; they came for the fish. And the fish were plentiful here. They cluttered the coves and filled the shoals that surrounded the Cape. But for the men, it was hard work getting them. It was wet, always wet, one of the wettest places. It was windy, too. Richard figured that when the wind came up here on the Cape, it was wilder than on the Grand Banks. That was his feeling, and it nagged at him whenever he fished here.

CHAPTER THIRTY-SEVEN

It was the evening of the twenty-fifth and the southeasterlies were manageable. Richard was alone on the *Mary Bernice*, waiting for the dorymen to return with their loads of fish. The old injury to his hand had been acting up, and young Captain James, who deferred to his experience and obvious seniority most of the time, told him to remain on board. He would take Richard's place in Dory Number 1 with Billy Reid. The Captain didn't have to argue, for Richard readily agreed. His finger throbbed. He recalled that there was supposed to be a cure in salt, a substance to which he'd been constantly exposed for the past few days, but that cure eluded him.

He was pleased, as was the young Captain, that the fishing was going well, that the pounds were filling with good fish in a reasonable time. They wouldn't be out here too long. Captain Paddy Walsh would be delighted with how his son's first trip as skipper had gone. Richard could return to his fledgling shore enterprise. Two of Mother Carey's chicks flew spasmodically by Richard as he stood at the stern of the *Mary Bernice*. The dark little birds were only seen at night, and most fishermen regarded them as good omens. Richard smiled at them.

*

Near midnight, a strong wind came out of the northeast. Richard had a feeling it was not solitary, but the beginning of a squall. He took down the sails as quickly as he could. Before long, though he could not know it, the force of the wind was felt all over the island, where it uprooted trees, flattened buildings, pulled up flakes and stages, and pushed telegraph lines to the ground. At sea, it was very soon clear that the *Mary Bernice* was in the middle of a gale – an August Gale.

The seas rose up to the railings of the *Mary Bernice* and then over them, dousing Richard in his oilskins and Kingfisher boots. Salt water splashed in his face as his eyes scanned the angry seas for any sign of the Captain and the dorymen. Then the midnight sky turned black and the rains began. The rains were merciless. They had to be flooding the dories. *If they can keep afloat*, Richard thought, *if they aren't capsizing or overturned*. He tried to remember if any of the dorymen could swim ... as if it mattered.

God, how long can they keep afloat in this? How far away are they? They were almost ready to come back to the schooner. They must have been on their way. They had been gone quite awhile already when this started.

The rains pounded the deck of the *Mary Bernice* as she wobbled to starboard, then to port, then back again, and again. Richard had thought she was a sturdy vessel, but she felt so light now, bouncing around on a swell that had grown cruel, and waves that towered over her and crashed down upon her. He was soaking wet, his oilskins rendered useless. He started to freeze as the salt water soaked the sweater coat he wore, and then his pants and underwear. How much time had passed? Where the hell were they? It got wetter still. The world was nothing but water. The noise was something fierce.

He saw something. It was getting closer. *Thank God, one of the dories.* But it wasn't a dory; it was too big, far too big. It was another schooner, very close, but being thrown around, too. He narrowed his eyes and recognized her: the *Jane and Martha*, out of Long Harbour. He could barely see someone who must be Captain James Bruce lashed to the wheel. The Captain was yelling at him, he could tell. He strained to hear the words. Captain Bruce seemed to be signalling him to get to port.

"My men! I'm waiting for my men!" Richard called back.

The Captain had assumed that and kept signalling him to head to safety. An older, experienced man, Captain Bruce had concluded that any dories and dorymen out in this were surely lost.

Then the *Jane and Martha* disappeared from Richard's view.

Panic began to rise from Richard's stomach, crawling up his chest, and into his throat. The contents of his stomach started to come up. Then he saw a vision of Angela, his unflappable wife, and he paused for a moment and breathed deeply. He would not be sick. He had to figure this thing out. The food he'd eaten stayed where it was.

Holding tight to the railings, he slowly made his way to the wheel and picked up the twine that was coiled alongside it, tied there lest it blow off. As the rain washed his face and the wind battered his body, he asked himself the question he was afraid to ask. He had to ask it. He was a family man; he wanted to live. *Should I go in? Should I try to make port?*

I might be able to. Captain Bruce seems to think I can make it. This is a good little schooner. She's new, well built. I'm not too far from St. Bride's. I could made a run for it.

Then he cast his eyes into the water, taking in its blackness and wildness, trying to will it back to some calm. *The men are out there, James and Billy and the rest. They're counting on me. I have to be here in case they come back. I can't leave them. How can I just leave them? I am their only chance.*

He gripped the wheel and sobbed into it like a baby.

He looked into the water again and let out a howl of anguish. They were lost, they had to be. How could they survive a gale like this? But how could he leave them? How could he walk back into Little Bay and look Michael Farrell's wife in the face? How could he ever speak to Billy Reid's mother?

But how could he leave his own wife a widow, a woman alone with young children? *I kicked my own son*, he cried, *that'll be his only memory of me.* He cursed himself and cried for his sin. Then he prayed as he lashed himself to the wheel and began to wait for his men to return.

They didn't come. In mockery of his vigil, the winds screamed and the rains flooded the schooner.

He stopped praying for the dorymen and began praying for himself, that he might live somehow. The rains poured down upon him and the winds blew his boat across unrelenting waves. Then the gale howled like never before and took the foremast and mainsail of the *Mary Bernice* with her. The rudder bashed against sunkers that rose out of the sea without warning.

Richard stuck his Kingfisher rubbers into the wheel so he wouldn't be swept out to sea. No longer was he waiting for the dorymen – now he was waiting for his God. He asked for forgiveness. Then he stopped praying for himself and prayed instead for Angela and his daughters and sons.

CHAPTER THIRTY-EIGHT

C oming only a few years after another memorable August Gale, the August Gale of 1935 was described by the Newfoundland newspapers as "the worst storm ever."

It caused destruction all over the island. In Westport, the government wharf was damaged and stages destroyed. Three dories were driven ashore at Burin, and twelve were lost between Corbin and Fox Cove, where four wharves and four stages were also destroyed. In St. Lawrence, five dories filled with gear were swept away. Four trap skiffs and six dories in Lamaline were destroyed, leaving many families there without the means to earn a living. Communities between Ship's Cove and Point Lance on the other side of Placentia Bay lost the forty dories and six motorboats that were the livelihood of 100 shore fishermen.

Bay de Verde, a community in Conception Bay North, suffered $1,000 of damages to fishing boats and property. The

Commissioner for Public Health and Welfare reported that the motorboats and gear of Edward Babb, Simeon Stone, and Alex Stone of Bryant's Cove were sunk and lost. In addition, Walter Drover, William Mercer, Joseph Mercer, and John Lundrigan of nearby Upper Island Cove each lost a boat.

At Northern Bay, in the same region, Henry Johnstone lost his stage; Patrick Howell and Richard Woodfine, their boats and engines. Two other men, Elias Woodfine and Joseph Woodfine, were luckier in that they lost their boats but recovered their engines. It was the same throughout Conception Bay. Six vessels sank at Holyrood. One of the most stricken places was Burnt Point, where thirty-two boats – thirteen motorboats and engines, eight small boats, five skiffs, three dories, and three motorboats – and the gear they contained were dashed to bits by the gale. The men who fished Baccalieu were robbed of a livelihood and handed a hungry winter instead.

The winds had come from the southeast and blew a hurricane into St. Mary's Bay farther south, not far from where Richard and the crew of the *Mary Bernice* fished. They veered to the southward at 4:00 A.M., continuing to blow strong. At Mosquito, St. Mary's Bay, huge waves tore away sections of the beach, wrecking stores, stages, and flakes, as well as fifty quintals of fish.

The *Laura Jane* of Musgrave Harbour on the Northeast Coast lost 300 quintals of fish. All over the island schooners were driven ashore by the winds and the waves. The *Norman Wareham*, skippered by Captain Blandford, was swept into the aptly named Wreck Cove near Lamaline, where her crew managed to scramble to safety. The crew of the *W.R. Power* survived when their schooner was driven ashore at Marysown. The *Gimball* from Harbour Buffett on

Long Island in Placentia Bay was wrecked at Riverhead in St. Mary's Bay, but her crew made it to land safe and sound.

The crew of the *Liberty*, a forty-five-ton vessel owned by the Snelgrove family, was lost at Barrow Harbour, Bonavista Bay. She burst one chain, dragged the other, then struck land, and sank in no more than fifteen minutes. Captain Reid of the *Valkyrie* rescued her crew.

In Renews, on the island's Southern Shore, the schooner *Bella Blanche* was damaged, as were several dories and motorboats. Several motorboats broke from their moorings at Clarenville and were wrecked when they drifted ashore. The government wharf at Bonavista was smashed in. Twelve telegraph lines between Badger and Grand Falls in Central Newfoundland blew down.

In St. John's, felt from the roof of O'Brien's Store on LeMarchant Road blew to the street below. Slates from the buildings on Water Street were strewn all over the street, carried there by the gale. The winds threw a power wire across an alarm wire, causing the fire alarm at the Central Fire Station to ring all night, lending an air of horror to the night. The gale uprooted trees in Bannerman Park, and in Quidi Vidi Village just outside the city; it cast down lightning that split two large trees in front of the Hennebury home. A miracle occurred when Robert Gulliver's house crashed to the ground while he slept and he was rescued by neighbours and the Royal Newfoundland Constabulary, entirely unharmed.

On the edge of the city, a bungalow under construction on the Newtown Road was lifted off its foundation by the storm and deposited eight feet away. The concrete blocks that had supported it were broken to bits.

The Doryman

The road to Octagon Pond in Conception Bay was criss-crossed with large fallen trees. It was the same with the Salmonier Line. The gale had caused a landslide at Crow Gulch between Curling and Corner Brook, on the island's west coast. It had reached a velocity of fifty-two miles per hour, according to the meterological station at Memorial College, ruining crops, downing wharves, stages, and flakes, flattening barns and out-buildings, and tearing roofs and chimneys off houses.

In Coachman's Cove, on the Northeast Coast, the storm cut a swath of destruction to the tune of $1,000 in fishermen's property alone. It tossed almost 600 cords of woods into the sea, carrying booms with it. It carried roads and bridges away and blew down a sawmill. It drove the schooner *Seabird*, loaded with lumber, ashore.

When the *Evening Telegram* and the *Daily News* reported these events on August 26, 1935, along with news of Italy's impending march into Ethiopia and debate about the fate of the Hapsburgs, readers were given no real clues about the great loss of life the gale had cruelly wrought.

187

CHAPTER THIRTY-NINE

The August Gale of 1935 left dozens of widows and orphans. With the gale of 1927 still fresh in memory, this time more than thirty Banks fishermen died.

The *Walter T,* skipped by Captain Boutcher of Kingwell, Placentia Bay was lost, as were her five crew members, four of them the Captain's brothers. Doryman James Wareham, a member of Captain James Hayden's crew, was swept overboard and drowned, six miles west of St. Mary's Quays. Doryman Abram Tibbo of the South Coast village of Pushthrough, fishing on the *Geneva Ethel*, was robbed of his life.

A Nova Scotia fisherman, Samuel Frank of Lunenburg, had been on the *Beatrice Beck* during the gale and was swept overboard in the high winds. The schooner was badly damaged and only able to limp into port when the seas had died down. Two Portuguese fishermen suffered broken legs. Their captain, José

Pinto, said that the storm was the worst he had ever seen in his twenty-five years on the Grand Banks.

The *Carrie Evelyn*, a forty-ton schooner skippered by Fred Mansfield of Hant's Harbour, ran aground at Fox Hole, Torbay. No trace of her Trinity Bay crew – Aeriel Green, Elias Soper, and Edgar Soper – was ever found.

The Administrator of the French islands of St. Pierre and Miquelon, just off the Burin Peninsula, was quick to offer his condolences to the Governor of Newfoundland. "I learn that considerable damage and loss of life was caused on the coast of Newfoundland by the storm," he wrote. The Governor thanked him and added that he feared the loss of life would turn out to be "heavy."

The omens observed by Lillian Walsh proved portentous. The crew of the *Annie Anita* were all lost, including Captain Paddy Walsh and his two young sons, Jerome and Frankie. Lillian's loss extended to James, her oldest son, and her nephew, both of whom had been on the *Mary Bernice* with Richard, as well as another nephew. From the *Annie Anita*, only the bodies of little Frankie and doryman Thomas Reid were recovered. The schooner had been seen drifting around Cape Pine, and the day after the gale she washed ashore at Hazel Cove near St. Shotts. Thomas and young Frankie were found buried in sand in the cabin, indicating that the storm had stirred up the bottom of the sea. Floating nearby were pieces of board marked *Walter T*; some of these were picked up at Portugal Cove South.

The ocean waters, almost cruelly calm now, were full of ghost ships. A schooner, bottom-up, floated silently by Cape Pine.

189

Another, also in total quiet, drifted on her beam ends. A third ghost ship with only one mast was seen off Powells Head.

Captain John Spurvey of the *Eleanor* arrived at Aquaforte with dories smashed up from the force of the gale. He said he was within sixty yards of a seventy-ton schooner about forty-five miles south of Ferryland Light. She was drifting eastwards with bare poles, her jib jumbo "in ribbons," and her foresail gone. The wind and rain wouldn't allow him to see her name, and she appeared to have no rudder.

As the days and then weeks passed, their men did not return. But they seemed to send signs. On August 30, wreckage from the *James and Mary* washed up at Southern Harbour, Placentia Bay. Trawls with the initials *WM* and *GW* on them washed ashore. On their way to the fishing grounds one morning, shore fishermen from the Battery in St. John's picked up a broom and water keg painted yellow.

A schooner plank bearing the name *Reginald Anstey* washed up at Baie Verte on the island's Northeast Coast. A yellow dory counter numbered "7" was recovered at Burnt Islands. Gear from the schooner *Eureka* was discovered at Herring Neck. Almost every day that fall, wreckage from the ghost schooners littered the beaches in Trepassey.

Right after the storm, the Newfoundland government sent the SS *Argyle* to the Virgin Rocks to investigate the wrecks reported there and the SS *Malakoff* to search around Trepassey and the Southern Shore. The *Malakoff* sighted only vessels that had floated aground; Captain Gosling's *Lottie Dunford*, a schooner owned by Captain Tobin of Trepassey, and another that belonged to one of the Inkpens of Burin. The ghost ships had disappeared.

It was as if they had never been there, as if Captain Spurvey and the others had merely dreamed of them in their nightmares.

Everywhere on the island, people scratched their heads. There had been nothing in the weather forecast to warn them of what was to come. At Friday midnight it read: "Moderate winds, partly cloudy and warm. Probably some showers over eastern portions at first." Then the report and forecast at noon Saturday, on the twenty-fifth, some hours before the gale began that night, read: "Pressure high and weather fair over Newfoundland except in extreme southeast portions where light rain has fallen. The indications were moderate variable winds with mostly good visibility, fair and warm."

The weather forecast for that day in the Canadian Maritimes had been more accurate and, had the Banks fishermen known of it, they would have rushed away from the fishing grounds and headed for the shelter of the bays. Reports in the *Halifax Herald* had warned of easterly to northeasterly winds and probably gales in "Maritime east," with winds increasing in the afternoon or night on the Grand Banks.

Reports in the St. John's *Daily News* estimated that the August Gale of 1935 caused damages totalling $45,510. Ten schooners were lost, worth a total of $23,000. Between ninety and 100 dories were gone, as were almost twenty small boats. Between twelve and fifteen marine engines were lost; so were twenty-five to thirty trap boats. Reports estimated that 1,000 quintals of fish were lost, but even this large number seems low, given that fish was lost from schooners, flakes, beaches, and onshore premises. Less than one-quarter of the losses were covered by marine insurance.

Prices had been low that year, so low that most fishermen required between twenty-five and fifty per cent more fish to equal the earnings of the year before. On the South Coast, the fishery was an almost total failure. Many families were facing a winter of destitution, even those with fathers and husbands still living.

The gale took the lives of dozens of Banks fishermen: men from Harbour Buffett, Kingwell, Petite Forte in Placentia Bay; Doctor's Cove and Pushthrough in Fortune Bay; Hant's Harbour in Trinity Bay; Lunenburg, Nova Scotia; and other coves and harbours where human lives and the sea were intertwined.

But the epicentre of human tragedy was Mortier Bay, home of sixteen of the dead men, and especially Little Bay. The small village had lost nine men and boys. Lillian Walsh, Captain Paddy's widow, lost no less than six of the men in her family: her husband, three sons, and two nephews. She mourned with Angela and her seven children, Billy Reid's mother, and Michael Farrell's wife and children, as well as the rest of the stricken village.

For many years, Captain James Bruce told the story of Richard Hanrahan refusing to abandon his men at the height of the windstorm. He told it with some sorrow, for he knew Richard's quest had been futile, if heroic. In one of many ironies and coincidences associated with the 1935 August Gale, years later, Captain Bruce's son Michael would marry Richard's youngest daughter Lizzie.

In another irony, the *Ronald W*, the large schooner that Richard could have sailed in but did not trust, successfully rode out the gale.

Meanwhile, Angela Hanrahan, a young woman with five children still at home, was left a widow with absolutely nothing at a time when she had least expected her husband to go to sea.

When the *Daily News* wrote a summary editorial on the 1935 fishery, it mentioned the low prices and the loss of the Italian markets. On the other hand, the new exporters' organization, the Saltfish Codfish Control Board, promised some stability in terms of marketing and prices. Sales to Portugal were increasing, the editorial read. It made no mention of the thirty fishermen who had died.

CHAPTER FORTY

The days went by, and there was no sign of Richard's body, nor of the *Mary Bernice* herself. Angela assumed the *Mary Bernice* and Richard had gone to the bottom of the sea. That was all she could do. She prayed, sometimes fearfully, that his death had not been a difficult or painful one.

There were only stories that people told over and over as if the constant telling could make some sense of what had happened. Angela's daughter Monnie, back from service in St. John's, talked of how she had bolted upright in her bed in the middle of the night of August 25 with a feeling of dread deep in her body. It had come as no surprise to her some days later when the priest from St. Patrick's parish in St. John's knocked on her door to confirm that her father's schooner was lost.

Angela's brother, Val Manning, told a story, too. He had been on board the *Tancook* safely moored in Little Bay during the gale and had awakened during the night to see Richard making a cup of tea for himself in the forecastle. The next morning, he sadly announced to Captain John Manning and the *Tancook's* dorymen, "You'll never see Dick again."

Angela heard that Albert Wareham over in Harbour Buffet was saying a twenty-ton schooner was bottom-up three miles off Haystack with a motorboat in tow. She was painted green, just as the *Mary Bernice* had been. In fact, the sighting was recorded in a newspaper report: "She apparently had an engine as propellor blades were over water. She had white balloon pole heads and the hull was under water. Spars were gone in three pieces and canvas gone." The vessel was a battered skeleton that somehow managed to limp along, if upside down. It did not occur to Angela that Richard's body might be aboard her, if in fact she was the *Mary Bernice*.

At the end of September, there was a kerfuffle at her door. It opened to reveal Rachel, and Father McGettigan, come all the way from the church in Marystown. The priest stood tentatively in the doorway; behind him was Sergeant Larry Dutton, equally grim-faced.

Angela motioned to her table and the chairs that surrounded it, all pine furniture that Richard had built. They came in and sat down. Rachel sucked in her breath. Then Father McGettigan handed Angela a letter.

Harbour Buffett, Placentia Bay
Sept. 25, 1935
W.W. Wareham & Sons

Dear Madam:

> *The following is a description of the body picked up on the Beach at Keating's Cove on the Eastern shore.*
>
> *Under the oil clothes was a sweater coat of greenish rug colour, darned on the side, also a pair of Kingfisher hip rubbers about size eight or nine.*

She remembered pulling the frayed threads of the sweater together with dark green wool that Rachel had carded that spring.

> *The shirt was of dark gray color, singlet was fleece lined, there was a pair of home-knit drawers and home-knit socks and vamps.*
>
> *As handy as I can go to an estimate of his weight would be about 170 pounds. He was a man of fairly short body thickly built. The middle finger on the right hand was crooked having apparently been broken at some time.*

Yes, she thought, *that's right, he hurt it at sea, crushed it under a block of ice in the hold.* The ice had slammed right onto it, he'd told her on his return home. He had winced dramatically to illustrate; he always had a bit of the performer in him.

> *On the body was a small calico bag containing religious articles. This was suspended about the neck and under the arm by a cord or tape of the same material. Attached to this was a small medal in a kid container, those were removed and others which had been blessed*

*were placed on the corpse. The reason for removal was for
identification purposes.*

She blinked hard. She couldn't read all the words, but she
recognized "medal" and she knew that St. Anne, the mother of
the Blessed Virgin Mary, had been with him to the last. She'd
given him the medal to replace the one he'd given to the poor
people of Port au Bras. She crossed herself hastily and uttered a
quick prayer that he had somehow felt St. Anne's comfort in it
all.

*The body was buried in the R.C. Cemetary at Port
Royal on Sept. 11, 1935.*

Respectfully submitted,
Thos. Davis, Constable
Harbour Buffett, Placentia Bay

She felt the salt of tears fill her eyes. In her throat, a lump
took shape and began to rise upwards. She stopped reading and
laid the thin piece of paper on the table for a minute. She tried
to let this horrible knowledge that he was really dead and his
death was final make its way into her brain, but her tears had
dried up and she felt numb. She was vaguely aware of Rachel's
bated breath a foot away. Then she shivered a little, remembering
that Richard had been Rachel's brother and that she would want
to know.

"It's him," she said, her voice filled with the powerlessness of
resignation and learned submission to God's will. "It's him."

"Oh God!" The voice was Rachel's. Angela herself let no noise out. Then Rachel's wailing filled the house and Father McGettigan, red-faced, rushed to the women's side. As Rachel howled, Angela peered down at the paper again.

P.S. A finger stall of calico was found inside the vest, in the vest pocket was a tin containing salve or catarrh powder, it was hard to tell which, however, it was in a Dr. Chase's catarrh powder box.

As long as Rachel wailed like that, there was no room for Angela's grief. Not here, not now. Besides, she felt that her grief was something between her and Richard. So she said nothing and folded up the paper. Then she pushed it down into her apron pocket. She couldn't help thinking of the ordinariness of it all: the salve for his injured finger, the new oilskins that he'd dipped in oil himself, the calico bag into which she'd inserted the medals, how they'd gotten them blessed at Lady Day in Oderin last year, the holes that he'd worn into the knees of his pants, and the patches she'd sewn on to cover them ...

"Angela," said Father McGettigan quietly. "The letter said he's been buried in Harbour Buffett – "

"No, Port Royal," she interrupted. Her attention to detail never left her, even now.

"The people there saw his medals and knew he was Catholic," said Sergeant Dutton, glad to have some useful information. "They waked him in the church."

"Yes, yes, on the island, I know, on the Catholic side, Port Royal." The priest was flustered now. He wasn't used to a new widow showing such a stone face. *It must be her Englishness*, he thought. Half of them from Oderin were English, whether they admitted it or not. Then he spoke again. "Should we arrange to have him taken back home to be buried here?"

Angela paused for a minute. Then she pursed her lips and said, "No, Father, he's fine there in Port Royal."

"But none of his own people are there," the priest objected. "He'll be all alone among strangers. It's not ..."

Angela's chest rose impatiently. "Leave him where he's to," she said firmly. "Leave him where he's to, he's been through enough."

EPILOGUE

Angela took her remaining children – Bride, Lizzie, Vince, Jack, and Patrick – to Oderin for the winter, where she lived with her family, the Mannings. She sold her house in Little Bay to a neighbour for thirty-five dollars.

Some weeks after Richard died, Angela received a bill from Baird's for his Kingfisher boots.

Richard's youngest daughter Lizzie had a particularly hard time recovering from her father's death. In what was probably an adaptation of a Micmac custom that she learned from her mother-in-law, Angela cut the child's long dark hair as a sign of mourning. Later she changed her daughter's name to Betty to signify that the mourning period was over.

In 1936, Angela moved her family to St. John's so that the boys could get the education their father wanted for them. She supported them through a small monthly allowance available for the widows and orphans of fishermen, and through her own unceasing hard work cleaning houses and doing laundry.

She outlived Richard by almost fifty years and died at ninety-four.

Richard's sister Rachel spent her whole life in Little Bay and died at age ninety-six.

Glossary of Newfoundland, Fishery, and Other Terms

Angelus: Catholic prayer to the Blessed Virgin Mary.

Arctic Screamer: Strong cold winds from the north or north-west, often following cold front.

Blackbacks: Greater black-backed seagulls, the largest gull of them all.

Chock: A large puncheon or cask to be used for fish processing (eg. As a liver butt) on board schooners.

Dory: A small flat-bottomed boat with flared sides and a sharp bow and stern. Dories were used extensively in both the shore and Banks fisheries in Newfoundland and Labrador.

Dory skipper: The man who owned the dory.

Fish: Cod; all other species of fish, such as salmon, were known by their proper names.

Flake: A platform built on poles and spread with boughs for drying fish.

Gale: A strong, forceful wind.

Ganger: A line spliced into a trawl. Steel hooks to catch fish were attached to the gangers.

Gurry: Fish offal, waste, usually fish innards. Banks fishermen never threw gurry back into the sea, which they regarded as a food basket.

Gurry kid: A large wooden pound that held the gurry.

Hagdown: Shearwater, a large bird frequently sighted at sea.

Lady Day: The fifteenth of August, the Feast of the Assumption. In some regions, the catch of cod brought in at the end of the summer was called the lady day fish.

Liver butt: A container used to render cod liver oil.

Micmac: This is the old-fashioned term for the indigenous people of Eastern Canada and the United States. It is derived from the term kin-friends. I use it here rather than the more current Mi'kmaq because it would have been used in the early 1900s.

Mizzling: This term is believed to have been coined by the naturalist Henry David Thoreau to describe the combination of thick mist and drizzle, a combination not unknown on the Banks. Its usage became common in New England and may have been picked up by Newfoundland fishermen who fished with Banks fishermen out of Gloucester, Massachusetts.

Mother Carey's chicks: Storm petrels, small dark-coloured seabirds, usually seen only at night.

Poultice: A soft moist mixture of meal, herbs, etc. spread on cloth and then applied to the body to bring about healing.

Pound: Types of enclosures used for the temporary holding of fish for or during fish processing.

Premises: Waterfront property, especially stores, wharves, and the flakes of merchants and fishermen.

Quintal: A hundredweight (112 lbs.), used as a measure for dried salt cod.

Rosary: Catholic prayer to the Blessed Virgin Mary.

Sails: The sails of a schooner included the mainsail, the largest, which weighed approximately 600 lbs.; the fore-sails – the balloon and jumbo – positioned ahead of the mainsail; and the staysail and foresail, positioned mid-ships (in the centre of the ship) like the mainsail.

Schooner: A large fishing vessel, from twenty tons to over 200 tons, associated with the Banks fishery, that travelled under sail.

Snow squall: A short, intense snowfall featuring strong winds.

Sou'wester: Waterproof fisherman's hat, broad-rimmed with side flaps, tied under the chin.

Squall: A sudden strong wind that disappears as quickly as it comes. Often it is a local storm.

Stage: An onshore platform which held working tables and sheds, etc. where women and men throated, gutted, salted, and otherwise prepared fish for drying.

Sunker: A submerged rock over which the sea breaks; they are sometimes difficult to see and therefore may be hazards to navigation.

Thwart: A seat across a boat, especially one used by an oarsman.

Tickle-ace: Black-legged kittiwake, a small but plentiful bird at Cape St. Mary's.

Tidal wave: The common name for the *tsunami* that hit the Burin Peninsula in 1929.

Token: A death omen, an apparition. Newfoundlanders believed that seeing a token of a loved one foretold the loved one's death within a year.

Trap skiff: A large fishing boat with no deck, propelled by oar, sail or small engine. Trap skiffs were used in the shore fishery, especially to haul cod traps.

Trawl: A buoyed line with baited hooks.

***Tsunami*:** The Japanese name for harbour wave. A subterranean earthquake, causing tidal action like that witnessed on Newfoundland's South Coast on November 18, 1929.

Turr: Common murre, hunted at sea. Also called the Baccalieu bird.

Water pups: Blisters caused by contact with salt water. One of the many occupational hazards of fishing, they usually develop on the wrist.

Western boat: A schooner-rigged fishing vessel between fifteen and thirty tons. Also called a Cape Boat. Western boats were usually away from port no more than a few days at a time.

List of Ships in *The Doryman*

Annie Anita: Built on the west coast of the island, a new schooner when she was lost, with her crew of seven, in the August Gale of 1935. Captained by Paddy Walsh of Little Bay.

Annie Healey: Nicknamed *Big Annie*, she was lost in the August Gale of 1927 just outside her home port of Fox Harbour. She had a crew of seven men.

Annie Jane: A western boat from Isle aux Morts on the island's Southwest Coast. She was lost in the 1927 August Gale and her crew of four died.

SS Argyle: A coastal boat. She did relief work on the Burin Peninsula after the 1929 *tsunami*. The Newfoundland Government also sent her to the Virgin Rocks to investigate reports of wrecks there after the August Gale of 1935.

Beatrice Beck: Samuel Frank of Lunenburg, Nova Scotia was swept overboard from this vessel during the August Gale of 1935.

Bella Blanche: Owned by the Brown family of Placentia Bay, she was damaged in Renews during the 1935 August Gale.

Bluenose: Famous Nova Scotia schooner constructed with steamed timber.

Bridget: Captain Paddy Manning's (the author's great grandfather's) schooner. The name of the actual vessel is lost to time, and Bridget being the name of the Captain's wife, it seemed a logical choice.

Cape Race: Fictional schooner trying to make port (Trepassey) during the August Gale of 1927.

Carrie Evelyn: A forty-ton schooner, captained by Fred Mansfield, that ran aground during the 1935 August Gale; her crew of four were lost.

SS Daisy: A revenue cutter. She did relief work on the Burin Peninsula after the 1929 *tsunami*.

Delight: The first recorded shipwreck off North America, at Sable Island, Nova Scotia in 1583.

Ella May: A schooner from Rencontre West in Fortune Bay lost in the August Gale of 1927; her crew of six perished.

Emma Jane: Fictional ship that the *Laura Claire* is berthed alongside in Burin during Richard's first trip.

Eureka: Her gear was discovered at Herring Neck near Twillingate after the 1935 August Gale, though the only vessel of that name on the Newfoundland schooner registry was a 1905 boat owned by a deceased individual.

Fair Haven: Fictional ship that the *Laura Claire* is berthed alongside in Burin during Richard's first trip.

Geneva Ethel: Doryman Abram Tibbo was swept overboard from this vessel and lost his life during the 1935 August Gale.

Gimball: Out of Harbour Buffet, Long Island, Placentia Bay she was wrecked at Riverhead, St. Mary's Bay during the August Gale, 1935.

SS Glencoe: A coastal boat. She did relief work on the Burin Peninsula after the 1929 *tsunami*.

Hilda Gertrude: A Rushoon schooner lost in the 1927 August Gale with a crew of seven.

James and Mary: Her wreckage washed up at Southern Harbour, Placentia Bay on August 30, 1935, five days after the gale.

Jane and Martha: Schooner out of Long Harbour, Placentia Bay, captained by James Bruce. She rode out the August Gale of 1935.

Jane Bailey: Fictional schooner trying to make port (Trepassey) during the August Gale of 1927.

Josephine Walsh: A fifty-three-ton schooner out of Little Bay.

Joyce M. Smith: A Nova Scotia two-masted schooner with a crew of twenty-two men lost in the 1927 August Gale.

Laura Claire: Fictional name of schooner that took Richard on his first trip to the Banks with his father. While the name of the actual vessel and her captain are lost to time, all other details are as true to family history as possible.

Laura Jane: A Musgrave Harbour vessel that lost 300 quintals of fish in the 1935 August Gale.

Liberty: Forty-five tons, she was lost at Barrow Bay, Bonavista Bay during the August Gale of 1935.

Lottie Dunford: Owned by Captain Tobin of Trepassey, she ran aground during the August 1935 Gale but was refloated by the *Malakoff*.

SS Malakoff: The Newfoundland Government dispatched her to search around Trepassey and the Southern Shore after the August Gale of 1935.

Mary Anne: Fictional schooner trying to make port (Trepassey) during the August Gale of 1927.

Mary Bernice: A western boat captained by James Walsh of Little Bay; first mate, Richard Hanrahan. Lost with five men in the August Gale of 1935.

SS *Meigle*: Coastal boat that visited the Burin Peninsula after the 1927 *tsunami*.

Norman Wareham: Captain Blandford's vessel was driven ashore at Wreck Cove, Lamaline in the August Gale of 1935.

SS *Portia*: The first radio-equipped vessel to reach the Burin Peninsula after the *tsunami* of 1929.

Ronald W: A Little Bay schooner captained by Jim Joe Farrell. Despite Richard Hanrahan's lack of faith in her age, she rode out the 1935 August Gale.

Sea Venture: The inspiration for Shakespeare's *The Tempest*, when she was wrongly presumed lost after an August Gale in 1609.

Seabird: A schooner loaded with wood driven ashore at Coachman's Cove during the gale of August 1935.

Tancook: Built in Nova Scotia by the builders of the *Bluenose*, the Mannings of Oderin bought her in 1924. She was forty tons and carried five dories.

Valkyrie: Captain Reid and the crew of the *Valkyrie* rescued the skipper and dorymen of the *Liberty* as she sank in the August Gale of 1935.

Vienna: A Burnt Island schooner with a crew of six men lost in the 1927 August Gale.

W.R. Power: A schooner driven aground at Marystown in the 1935 August Gale.

Walter T: Lost during the August Gale of 1935; dead were Captain Boutcher, his four brothers, and one other doryman.

DEATHS IN THE *TSUNAMI* (TIDAL WAVE) OF 1929*

James Lockyer, Allan's Island
Thomas, Henry, and Elizabeth Hipditch, Point au Gaul
Elizabeth Walsh, Point au Gaul
Thomas Walsh, Point au Gaul
Mary Anne Walsh, Point au Gaul
Thomas Hillier, Point au Gaul
Irene Hillier, Point au Gaul
Elizabeth Hillier, Point au Gaul
Bridget Bonnell, Taylor's Bay
The child of Robert Bonnell of Taylor's Bay
John and Clayton Bonnell, Taylor's Bay
The child of George Piercey, Taylor's Bay
Frances Kelly, Kelly's Cove
Mrs. Kelly's daughter, Dorothy, Kelly's Cove
Jessie Fudge, Port au Bras
Gertrude Fudge, Port au Bras
Hannah Fudge, Port au Bras
Harriet Fudge, Port au Bras
Henry Dibbon, Port au Bras
Louisa Brushett Allan, visiting her brother Henry Dibbon, Port au Bras
Mary Ann Bennett, Port au Bras
Sarah Rennie, Lord's Cove, and her children:
Rita Rennie, Lord's Cove
Patrick Rennie, Lord's Cove
Bernard Rennie, Lord's Cove

* This list is intended as a memorial to those who died, but it may not be complete due to the inadequacies of the historical record.

Some Dorymen, Mates, and Captains lost in the prosecution of the Newfoundland Banks Fishery*

Andrew Barnes, Fortune Bay, *Joyce M. Smith*, 1927.
Fred Barnes, Fortune Bay, *Joyce M. Smith*, 1927.
Captain Boutcher, Kingwell, *Walter T*, 1935.
Four Boutcher Brothers, Kingwell, *Walter T*, 1935.
John Brinton, *Annie Anita*, 1935.
Patrick Bruce, *Annie Healey*, 1927.
Charles Burbridge, Epworth, *Joyce M. Smith*, 1927.
George Burbridge, Epworth, *Joyce M. Smith*, 1927.
Dan Cheeseman, Rushoon, 1927.
Philip Cheeseman, Burin Bay Arm, *Joyce M. Smith*, 1927.
Robert Cheeseman, Burin Bay Arm, *Joyce M. Smith*, 1927.
Edward Cheeke, *Annie Anita*, 1935.
Samuel Crocker, Creston South, *Joyce M. Smith*, 1927.
Arthur Dominick, Belloram, *Joyce M. Smith*, 1927.
James Farewell, *Joyce M. Smith*, 1927.
Thomas Samuel Farewell, *Joyce M. Smith*, 1927.
Michael Farrell, Little Bay, *Mary Bernice*, 1935.
John Foley, *Annie Healey*, 1927.
Samuel Frank, Lunenburg, N.S., *Beatrice Beck*, 1935.
Ariel Green, *Carrie Evelyn*, 1935.
James Hancock, Pool Cove, Fortune Bay, *Joyce M. Smith*, 1927.
Murdock Hancock, Pool Cove, Fortune Bay, *Joyce M. Smith*, 1927.
Benjamin Hannaram (Probably Hanrahan), *Joyce M. Smith*, 1927.
Charles Hanrahan, Little Bay, *Annie Anita*, 1935.
Richard Hanrahan, Little Bay, *Mary Bernice*, 1935.
James Hodder, *Joyce M. Smith*, 1927.
Thomas Hodder, *Joyce M. Smith*, 1927.
Archibald Keating, Salt Pond Burin, *Joyce M. Smith*, 1927.
John Kelly, *Annie Healey*, 1927.

James King, *Annie Healey*, 1927.

Dennis Long, Fox Cove, *Mary Bernice*, 1935.

Fred Mansfield, Captain, Hant's Harbour, *Carrie Evelyn*, 1935.

Edward Maxner, Lunenburg, N.S., *Joyce M. Smith*, 1927.

William Maxner, Lunenburg, N.S., *Joyce M. Smith*, 1927.

George Mitchell, *Annie Anita*, 1935.

John Mullins, Captain, Fox Harbour, Placentia Bay, *Annie Healey*, 1927.

Michael Mullins, Fox Harbour, Placentia Bay, *Annie Healey*, 1927.

John Pike, *Joyce M. Smith*, 1927.

Thomas Poole, Belloram, *Joyce M. Smith*, 1927.

Billy Reid, Little Bay, *Mary Bernice*, 1935.

Thomas Reid, Little Bay, *Annie Anita*, 1935.

Charles Sampson, *Annie Healey*, 1927.

Elias Soper, *Carrie Evelyn*, 1935.

Edgar Soper, *Carrie Evelyn*, 1935.

Abram Tibbo, Pushthrough, *Geneva Ethel*, 1935.

Dominic Walsh, Little Bay, *Annie Anita*, 1935.

Frankie Walsh, Marystown, *Annie Anita*, 1935.

James Walsh, Captain, Marystown, *Mary Bernice*, 1935.

Jerome Walsh, Marystown, *Annie Anita*, 1935.

Patrick Walsh, Captain, Marystown, *Annie Anita*, 1935.

James Wareham, 1935.

James Warren, Salt Pond Burin, *Joyce M. Smith*, 1927.

Samuel Warren, Salt Pond Burin, *Joyce M. Smith*, 1927.

John Whalen, Fox Cove, Burin, *Joyce M. Smith*, 1927.

*While this list is intended to serve as a memorial to lost Banks fishermen, it is no way comprehensive; a complete list would include hundreds of names over many decades rather than the fifty-eight included here.

Acknowledgements

This book came about because of the participation of many people. First of all, I wish to offer my deepest thanks to my husband Paul Butler. It is no exaggeration to say that without Paul's encouragement and input this book would not exist.

Thanks are also due to Garry Cranford, Margo Cranford, Jerry Cranford, and everyone at Flanker Press for their keen interest, and unflagging dedication and professionalism; my cousins Colleen Hanrahan, John Abbott, Art and Janice Cheeseman, Anne Spollen, and especially my aunt Jean Hanrahan.

I am deeply grateful to my uncle, Vince Hanrahan, who was story consultant on this manuscript; my late cousins Jim, Steve, and Jerry Abbott; my late father, Patrick; my late aunt Monnie Cheeseman; my late aunt Elizabeth Bruce; and my aunt Bride Piazza; all of whom brought Richard, Steve, Elizabeth, and the rest of the family so vividly into my life for many years through their reminiscences and stories.

I am particularly indebted to my late great-aunt Rachel Hanrahan Abbott and my late grandmother Angela Manning Hanrahan. It was my privilege to hear first-hand from these spirited women the stories of their lives, stories that reached into the 1890s.

I also owe a debt of gratitude and much inspiration to several Newfoundland writers: Cassie Brown, author of *Death on the Ice* and *Standing Into Danger*; the compilers of the *Encyclopedia of Newfoundland and Labrador* and the *Dictionary of Newfoundland English*; Otto Kelland, author of *Dories and Dorymen* and the hauntingly beautiful hymn, "Let Me Fish Off Cape St. Mary's"; Dr. Leslie Harris, author of *Growing Up with Verse: A Child's Life in Gallows Harbour* and a number of lovingly written articles on Placentia Bay; Percy Janes, author of one of Newfoundland's greatest novels, *House of Hate*; and meteorologist Bruce Whiffen for his fine series of articles on the weather of Newfoundland and Labrador.

Last but not least, I would like to thank the Newfoundland and Labrador Arts Council, and Word on the Street, Halifax, Nova Scotia.

ABOUT THE AUTHOR

Maura Hanrahan is the winner of the 2003 Lawrence Jackson Award for writing, administered by the Newfoundland and Labrador Arts Council. Her latest book is *Tsunami: The Newfoundland and Labrador Tidal Wave Disaster*.